Borderlands

Borderlands

Western Stories

JANE CANDIA COLEMAN

Five Star • Waterville, Maine

Published in 2001 by arrangement with Golden West Literary Agency.

G.K. Hall Large Print Western Series.

The text of this Large Print edition is unabridged.
Other aspects of the book may vary from the original edition.

Set in 16 pt. Plantin.

Printed in the United States on permanent paper.

Library of Congress Cataloging-in-Publication Data

Coleman, Jane Candia.
    Borderlands : western stories / Jane Candia Coleman.
      p.   cm.
    Originally published: Unity, Me. : Five Star, 2000.
    ISBN 0-7838-8727-2 (lg. print : hc : alk. paper)
   1. Western stories.   2. Large type books.
PS3553.O47427 B6 2001
813′.54—dc21   2001039239

Table of Contents

Foreword

That I chose *Borderlands* as a title for this collection was as much due to the psychological aspects of the word as to the physical ones. The setting for many of these stories is the U.S./Mexico border, the country where I live, and the place where so much of our Western history has unfolded. In addition, there are the mental barriers and crossings that take place within any story.

Set in Nebraska, "Sandhill Cranes," is a story of migrations, not only of the long flight of cranes, but of the equally long and perilous journeys of the children on the orphan trains that ran from New York to the West from 1854–1929. Most of these orphans were adopted into good homes. But some, like Delia, were not.

"Loner" takes place on Montana's border with Canada at a time when greed and the absence of law made settlement difficult and often intolerable for those in search of a new and better life, and who were forced to fight for that life and for their belief in possibility.

Louisa Houston Earp was the common-law wife of Morgan Earp, Wyatt's younger brother who was murdered in Tombstone. For more than a century after his death, she was only a shadow figure known as Lou. Her letters, generously provided by her family to Earp historian Glenn Boyer, reveal her travels and something of her life with the Earps, but little of the woman who wrote them. My first few readings of these letters left me unimpressed. I had, in fact, decided that the beautiful Lou was quite dull, until I realized that she was a product of her day — a mid-Victorian woman unused to discussing her feelings or thoughts and shaped by the culture of her times. Judging by what she mentions of her sisters' letters to her, many women communicated in what amounted to a separate language — the language of flowers, perhaps a metaphor for themselves — and thus the story, "Wild Flower," in which I have mingled fictional letters with those actually written by Louisa.

"The Fiddle Case" is a true story — one that might have ended in tragedy. Jerusha Stiles gives birth to a daughter while in a wagon train bound for California. When the child apparently dies under mysterious circumstances, the bereaved mother cannot admit the fact of death and refuses to bury her child in the desolate country of the Cimarron Cut-Off. Meelie, a medicine woman, realizes that the child is simply in a catatonic state and reawakens her. When I was first told this story, I immediately wondered what the feelings of the mother were, what she thought and saw as she looked out of the wagon and made her stubborn and fortunate decision. These small details are, to me, the stitchings in

8

the quilt that is the history of the West.

"Borderlands," the title story, comprises many journeys, a multitude of crossings, not the least of which is Pancho Villa's raid on Columbus, New Mexico, an act of unprecedented daring by a most unusual revolutionary leader, and one that is witnessed by a trio of unusual travelers — two artists who discover the beauty of the West, and a journalist on an assignment that turns out to be more than he imagined.

The vigor and frequency with which people of the 19th and early 20th Century traveled has always amazed me. Likewise, the fact that so many of our Western outlaws sought sanctuary in South America and lived there to what is known as a "ripe old age." "A Pair to Draw to" is another story based on fact — how the wives of two famous outlaws left South America and came to the border country to open a sanatorium to "bilk rich old men," in the words of historian John Tanner — who first told me the story with a twinkle in his eye.

This desert country where I live is both beautiful and tragic. Tragic because of the very fragility of the environment. "The Perseid Meteors" is a double love story — the love between the two main characters, and the love both they — and I — have for the mystique of place.

Cowboys have never been noted for their intellects, but what they are, almost to a fault, is honest, loyal, and true. And so, Nolo Pearce in "Rodeo" proves his mettle in his fight to regain

9

his son. Bless him. My admiration for Nolo, his sidekick, Merle, and all those like them is boundless.

With "Marvel Bird," the collection ends as it began, with an abused woman summoning courage from the great, beating heart of a horse. In my opinion, there is nothing that surpasses the message to be learned from the least of horses.

Sandhill Cranes

Although he was in a hurry to get home before dark, at the sight and sound of the migrating cranes Sam Warner pulled up his team and sat, head tilted up to the sky. Where they came from, where they were going, he didn't know, but their arrival each year was a harbinger of spring, a part of the mystery of the land and its cycles that satisfied him in some way he couldn't define, a beauty that was both promise and the fulfillment of promise, complete in itself. He sat on the wagon seat, reins held loosely, and watched as they flew, more birds than he could count, darkening the sky, filling the air with a crying that was like the baying of far away hounds.

The filly he had bought, that was tied to the back of the wagon, caught the excitement and snorted and danced as if she, too, wished to take to the air, a wind-borne leaf.

"It's a sight, isn't it?" he said to her. "Makes you wish. . . ." His voice trailed off. What *was* it he wished, that caught in his throat, a longing so huge it couldn't be dislodged, a wildness like the river when it flooded its banks? He shook his head to bring himself back to earth. A busy man, who bred some of the finest horses in the state, he had no time for foolishness or introspection.

11

"Best get home." He tightened the reins, and the team moved out, quickly now, headed for the barn. And then, where the lane curved and began its ascent, he saw a woman, her blue skirt billowing as she walked, so that she seemed to be dancing, as light as one of the cranes, as a seed of milkweed drifting on air. She was tall, with long arms, and a braid of dark hair that hung past her hips and swayed with her motion, and for a moment Sam thought she was a ghost, flickering at the edge of vision like foxfire.

But the horses had pricked up their ears and were watching, ready to shy away from the apparition, from the flutter of a blue skirt where it did not belong.

"Easy now." His voice sounded loud to him, out of place, as if he had broken a spell, ripped through the luminous fabric of a dream and, without intention, ruined perfection. He saw that the woman was walking unsteadily, and what he'd thought was a dance was actually a reaching out with one long arm in a vague attempt to balance herself.

He drew alongside, bent down, said — "Ma'am?" — like a question, and she turned, looked up out of eyes the gray-green color of river water. One half of her face was pale as milk, the other was bruised, lop-sided, the eye swollen shut.

He stepped down and caught her as she fell, amazed at the lightness of her, skin over hollow bones, stick, blade of grass, small bird left behind in the great wave of migration.

Not dead, he thought, simply worn out and in obvious pain. Carefully he laid her in the wagon bed, covered her with an old horse blanket, then stood looking at her and frowning. She was younger than he'd thought at first, neither child nor woman, and the half of her face that was unmarked was delicately made, a mockery of its grotesque twin.

His fingers curled into fists; the anger that always erupted in him at brutality to the small, the helpless, blurred his vision. "Damn him to hell, whoever he was!"

Abruptly he got back on the seat and took up the reins, knowing that Sybil, his mother, would heal the girl's wounds and find out the truth if anyone could, for she had a way with her, magic in her hands, her voice, and, like this girl, had once come alone and unwanted into the country that she now loved with a passion.

Five years old, wearing a dress that was too small, a coat that was too big, a bonnet with frayed ribbons tied beneath her chin, Sybil stepped off the orphan train onto the station platform and stood, a part of her wishing she was back within the safety of the orphanage walls, another part waiting to be noticed, to be taken in and loved.

Lucy Warner hadn't gone to town in search of a child or a servant. She'd spent the morning at the horse fair, buying and selling with the shrewdness for which she was famous, and her way home took her past the station where the train sat, puffing and billowing steam, and the children, row after row of them in ill-fitting clothes, stood still, stricken into silence by the strange surroundings.

"Who are all those kids? Why are they here?" Twelve-year-old Jake stared at the pale faces, the hopeful eyes.

"Poor things." His mother's voice was sad. "They're orphans. Sent out to be adopted, and a good thing, too, seeing how they look. Half starved, some of them."

Tough and shrewd as she was in a horse trade, Lucy hid a heart soft as butter — or thought she did. Her husband, Ned, and the animals she raised knew the truth, but kept it to themselves.

One of the children, a little girl, was staring at her from under the brim of a much-worn bonnet, and staring at the team she drove with what seemed like admiration.

Lucy pulled up sharply. "Wait here," she said to Jake, and leaped down in a swirl of skirts.

"You like my horses?" she asked the girl without preamble.

The child nodded, her face expressionless. More out of fear than stupidity, Lucy thought to herself. She stooped down to the girl's level. "What's your name?"

"Sybil. . . . ma'am."

"Pretty." Lucy smiled. "And how old are you, Sybil?"

A faint smile flickered in response, then faded, replaced by a frown. "I think . . . I think I'm five. Nobody knows for sure. Do you . . ." — she swallowed hard and forced the next words — "do you want a little girl, ma'am?"

Did she? If not, what was she doing here putting hope into a strange child's head? After Jake, she had been unable to conceive, a fact that hadn't worried her unduly. Until now. A woman should have a daughter, she thought. Not so much to pass on blood-lines, as to inherit knowledge, to act as both mirror and companion, sharer of secrets and laughter, joy and sorrow — all those womanly things that could not be spoken to a man, even one's husband.

Instinctively, the way she did most things, Lucy held out her hand. "Would you like to come home with me?"

Sybil, who had been holding her breath, took hold with icy fingers. "If you please," she said.

Her sigh of relief broke Lucy's heart, but, all business once more, she set off down the platform in search of the mayor, the parson, the worthy gentlemen of the orphan committee who would sign the girl over.

She expected no difficulty, nor did she encounter any. Lucy and Ned Warner were respected citizens, churchgoers, albeit irregularly, upstanding folk who owned the biggest ranch in the county. Not all of the children would be as fortunate. Some would be made into little more than slaves, others ill-fed, made fun of, allowed to remain uneducated. Although the committee tried its best, there were more failures than were talked about, but with Lucy Warner there was no hesitation.

15

"Reckon you know the rules, Miz Warner." Harry Jenks, the mayor, smiled over his spectacles. "She gets sent to school, brought up God-fearing, raised like your own."

Lucy looked down her nose at the little man. "That goes without saying."

As she'd intended, he groveled. "I'm just obligated to say it. No offense. If you'll just sign this paper here."

She did, with a flourish, then took Sybil's hand and walked back toward Jake and the wagon and team.

Jake knew his mother as well as he knew himself. "You got an orphan!" he exclaimed.

"She's your sister now," Lucy said, giving him a look that told him plainly to behave.

His face split in a grin. "I always wanted a sister." It was the truth. He'd been, at times, lonely, his parents involved with each other, with the horses, leaving him on the outside wishing for someone his age to talk to, to roam the river and hills with. Except he hadn't imagined a girl, especially not one like this one, in her ill-fitting clothes and eyes the color of leaves seen underwater. Still, there was a look about her, as if she was lost but would stand her ground, somebody he'd like at his back in a fight, even if she was a girl and little. And, besides, it must have taken courage to get on that train and go alone to a place she'd never seen.

He handed the reins to his mother and grinned again, showing the gap where his teeth were slow in coming. "I'm Jake. I reckon we'll be friends, you and me."

16

The girl looked at him a long time, taking his measure, assessing her place in this new world, among strangers, and he found he was holding his breath hoping she'd accept him. When it came, her smile was cautious, shimmering in her eyes and spreading demurely to her lips. She said: "My name's Sybil. I came from New York. Bet you never been there."

He stood on his heritage and his pride. "And you never seen a ranch and horses like we got, either."

She bowed her head. "No. But I guess I'm about to. I guess you'll show me. Won't you?" The eyes flicked up, caught his, and held them.

"Somebody's got to," he said, his voice on the edge of change, gruff.

"Is there snakes?" she asked, clutching her hands tightly in her lap. In her whole life, she'd never seen a snake, but she'd heard about them, and it was necessary to know, to be prepared for the worst.

Lucy looked out of the corner of her eye. "Don't scare the poor mite."

"Some," Jake said, sitting up straight. "But you don't have to worry. I won't let 'em get you."

"What if you aren't there?" She clasped her fingers tighter.

"I'm always there," he said.

Sybil fit into the tightly knit family without a ripple, grateful and knowing what was required as if she'd been taught since her birth. She had a way with animals, particularly the horses, moving around them without fear, filled with kindness and the sense of authority that bred obedience and trust.

"A Gypsy," Ned called her, seeing her with his prize stallion. "You've gone and brought us a Gypsy."

Lucy snorted. "Not with that hair. Not with those eyes. She's just born with the touch, thank God, and don't pretend you're not glad I found her. We're lucky."

"For how long?" In Ned's experience, girls got married young and left home to start their own family. Better sons, he thought. Better Jake, steady as a rock and made for the place.

Lucy watched as the girl talked to the big stallion that lowered its head over the fence and nickered softly. Once again, she blessed her instinct. "Don't worry," she said, smiling to herself. "Wherever she's from, whoever she is, she's home now, and she's not leaving. Mark my words."

In the spring when Sybil was eighteen, she and Jake fell in love, or perhaps, as she said later, she'd loved him from the first day and didn't know it. Abandoned at birth, left on the doorstep of a church, taken in, taken care of, she had never been taught about love until it caught up with her, hit her smack in the face, and left her stunned.

What she remembered most about the day she arrived was the fear in the pit of her stomach, the sheer terror that she would be left, standing on the platform, unwanted and alone. Even the orphanage was better than being abandoned a second time, in a strange place, in a town that had only a few streets, and where the wind swooped across the prairie like

18

the hot breath from a fierce and unseen animal.

The sight of Lucy Warren's horses, blue-black and shining, had taken her mind off herself for a blessed moment, and then there was Lucy coming toward her in that no-nonsense way she had, boot heels thudding, her eyes quick and bright in the shadow of her old felt hat, and there had been Jake offering his friendship, blustering a little, but the orphanage had been full of boys and their bluster, and he wasn't nearly as frightening as the thought of being left.

She had fallen asleep on the way home, and she didn't wake until they came around the bend, and she saw the house, white and welcoming, the big barn, the pastures where horses were grazing, their coats glossy in the long rays of the evening sun. It was like a picture in a book — or a dream — a place out of a fairy tale to her who had only known the drab walls of the orphanage, the hardness of city streets. Her starved little heart, that only a few hours before had seemed turned into ice, began to beat like a drum, like the rhythm of the hoofs of the horses.

"Oh." It was a breath, a muted sigh.

Lucy looked down, saw the child's face flushed with what looked like tears in her magnificent eyes.

"It's home," she said gently. "From now on."

And in that place Sybil had bloomed, grown strong and swift, and sure of herself, learned the people and the life, and found that she had the gift of healing in her hands, a magic in her touch.

At eighteen she stood in a pasture, grateful for what had been given to her. Why? She didn't know, didn't have time to wonder. She had come for the mare that was due to foal, and that approached, nickering softly. She put her arms around the slender neck, touched the swollen belly, and then she heard it, the far-off music of the cranes, and the music was wild, lonely, a pouring out of sound that made her ache, for what she couldn't tell. Mare and girl stood listening, waiting for the birds to come, an irregular ribbon of dark bodies and wings, a thousand arrows piercing the invisible air.

"It's a sight, isn't it?" Jake spoke from behind her.

She jumped, brought back by his voice into her body. "I always forget," she said. "And then they come, and it's like the first time, only different. It makes me feel. . . ."

She stopped, searching for words that wouldn't come, aware of the fact that Jake was no longer her childhood companion but a man grown a head taller than she, with serious dark eyes that held the miracle of the birds in them, and the reflection of the sky.

"What?" he asked. "What do you feel?"

She looked down at herself, feet planted firmly when they wanted to take wing. "Like . . . like something's missing," she said finally. "Oh, I don't mean in the house, or with anybody here. It's something else, and I don't know what it is or how to find it."

He ran a hand over the mare's neck, a man's hand but gentle. "You remember the day you came?"

She nodded, watching his fingers. "I thought I'd come to heaven. And I never changed my mind."

He smiled, and for a moment she saw him as a boy, gap-toothed and blustering. "I figured I'd found what I'd been missing. A friend," he said.

"Me, too."

His hand lay still. "I didn't figure I'd want more. But I do."

She understood because she knew him, had from the first, because she had grown to the land and its cycles like the mare standing patiently beside them, and suddenly she knew that the ache inside her could not be healed except by another.

"That's good then." It came out a whisper, and was not what she wanted to say at all.

His head jerked up. "You mean that?"

She saw the boy, saw the man, looked back across the years, and saw the truth. "Since that first day. I was scared, and you were nice. You're nicer now, though."

"And you're prettier."

She was pleased. "See," she said. "Back then you used to call me 'Tadpole.' "

He reached out and swung her in his arms. "Some things change," he said. "And other things stay the same. Like those birds. Like you and me. But it's all of a piece when you think about it."

And that was the wonder of it — the flowing of life, the loving, the labor, the times when she sat stitching the years together, telling her story to her own son, Sam, the boy who himself had become a man with a past and a future not yet written.

Sam Warner turned into the yard and found his mother and Will Flanagan their foreman in the corral with a yearling. Seeing Sam, Sybil came through the gate, dusting her hands.

"He'll make a fine horse in another year," she said. "And the cranes are back."

"I found a woman in the lane. She's hurt. You better come." Sam ignored his mother's greeting and turned to the wagon bed, while Sybil stood for a second, jolted by a feeling of recognition, as if this scene had happened before and she'd been a part.

"Who?" she asked.

"I don't know, but she's hurt. She fainted. One minute she was walking along, and then she wasn't. I thought . . ." — he frowned, remembering — "I thought she was a ghost."

"No such thing." Sybil climbed into the wagon as if she were still seventeen. "Why!" her voice rose over the boards, "why she's just a girl! Who did this?"

He shrugged, sure he'd not seen anyone else — an attacker in the trees, strange tracks on the road. Except he'd been watching the cranes, his thoughts far away — the cranes and the girl he'd thought was dancing.

"Is it bad?" he asked, giving up on explanation.

"Bad enough, but there's a pulse. Her shoulder's dislocated. Take her in and put her on my bed. I'll see if I can't get it back in place before she wakes up."

He did as he was told, feeling a sense of relief as he mounted the steps and went into the familiar rooms. In an odd way, he had expected them to be changed, and all because of the girl who lay in his arms, a foreign element in the order of his existence.

When his father died, he and Sybil had gone on as they always had, raising fine horses, each allowing for the emptiness that was within the other. It was perhaps Sybil who had sustained the greater loss, a lifetime friend, a husband, but Sam had grieved for the father he'd known for such a short time, knowing he himself could never take his place. Eventually, however, mother and son had achieved a rhythm that was their own, a communication that hadn't so much to do with words as with what they knew had to be done, and it was soothing to them both.

He put the girl down carefully on the old spool bed that had been Lucy Warner's, and pulled the coverlet over her, thinking that, in the morning, he'd go back to town, ask around, find out where she had come from. Surely she belonged somewhere. Surely her absence had caused someone grief.

Sybil came in carrying a pan of water that smelled of herbs. "Go see to that filly," she said. "Maybe she should stay in the barn tonight. She's a dandy, though. Must have cost you."

"Not what you'd think. The folks who had her were headed west and needed money."

"Some folks can't see the forest for the trees." She wrung out a cloth and turned to the girl on the bed. "Poor thing. No hat, no coat, beaten for

God knows what reason, and wandering around with rain coming on. Makes you wonder."

"It does." He felt his anger stir again. "Who'd do it?"

"Nobody decent." She bent down, smoothed the dark hair off the girl's forehead, and felt her heart turn over. What had happened to this child could have happened to her, but fate had directed otherwise — fate and Lucy Warner who'd gone by her instinct and who'd taught her to trust her own.

"Go on now," she said. "I'll do what I can."

By the time Sam came in from the barn, she was taking a pan of biscuits out of the oven.

"How is she?"

"Asleep. I got her shoulder back and put salve on those bruises. Might be a bone in her face broken. I couldn't tell." She sighed. "Wash up."

"Did she say anything? Her name or where she's from?"

"Not a word." And that bothered her — the look in the girl's eyes when she'd come to for a moment. There was intelligence and then blankness, as if a curtain had been drawn between two parts of a whole.

He dried his hands, rolled down his sleeves, and came to the table. "Guess I'll go back to town tomorrow. Maybe somebody's looking for her."

"And maybe that somebody's the one who did it to her. We'll just keep her till we find out. Besides, she's in no shape to be going anywhere."

24

"She made it here."

Sybil rested her chin on her hands and looked at him. "And that's a mystery. There's no way she could've walked from town. No hat, no shawl, blisters all over her feet. Makes me wonder."

He'd wondered, too, and come up with nothing. "We can't just keep her."

"Oh, yes," she answered softly. "Oh, yes, we can. I don't want it on my conscience that we turned her out. And, besides, I've got a feeling."

He knew about his mother's feelings. You didn't fight them, just let life go on and hope things turned out like she said. Usually, they did. Now, though, he wasn't sure.

The first drops of rain spattered on the roof, and Sybil cocked her head, listening. "Funny," she said, "how the girl and the cranes came at the same time. It seems my whole life's been marked by those birds."

"You're making a judgment about nothing," he told her.

"And you sound like your father. You men ought to listen once in a while. There's a reason for everything."

He took a mouthful of biscuit, washed it down with hot coffee. "Charity is as good a reason as any. I wasn't about to leave her on the road. Her or anybody else."

Annoyed, she drummed her fingers on the table. "All I'm saying is, let's not go off half-cocked. Let's hear what she has to tell us before we do anything."

After all, there was sense in what she said. He nodded agreement and reached for another biscuit.

She lay curled up, hugging her body to herself, a pathetic defense but all she'd ever had. A lamp on the bureau cast a low light, and she could hear voices coming from another room. She listened, hoping to make out what was being said, but the words ran together in a blur of sound that was as foreign as the kindness in the woman's hands had been.

In the morning, she thought, she would leave this place and go on, find a city where she could lose herself in a crowd, find work, any kind. She wasn't choosy. For now, the bed was soft, and she was tired, and it was safe to close her eyes and drift away. Safe. She pondered the word, turned it around in her head examining the feeling, the comfort of the bed, the yellow light of the lamp. Safe. But for how long? She closed her eyes and slept.

The crying of the birds woke her, and she lay still, listening, wondering for a moment where she was. From somewhere came the smell of breakfast cooking, bacon frying in its own fat, bread rich with yeast baking in an oven, and her mouth began to water. She was always hungry, but never as much as now, lying in a comfortable bed, wearing a nightgown that hinted of luxury she'd never dreamed of.

With a struggle, she sat up, waited for the dizziness to pass before she stood and looked for her clothes. All she found were her boots, shabby broken things that looked as if she'd walked a thousand miles. In a way, she had. She felt she'd been walking forever, the horizon always drawing away, hope and courage discarded at the side of the trail along with ten years of life.

Were they looking for her now, Pa and Beeler? Had they been able to follow the looping path she'd taken, not so much on purpose as out of the nightmare of pain and fright? She shook her head to blot out the horror, and the abrupt movement made the dizziness come back so she held to the windowsill, bent over as if she were old.

"You're awake!" Sybil's cheerful voice startled her, and automatically she flattened herself against the wall.

Sybil caught the gesture, read the fear in the girl's eyes, and muttered a curse, but when she spoke, all she said was: "It's only me. Sybil Warner. My son Sam found you last night. Do you remember?" She shook her head, slowly this time, and closed her eyes, and Sybil went on. "Just as well. Your shoulder was dislocated. I got it put back right, and I've got some clothes you can borrow. Breakfast's nearly ready. Hungry?"

A nod. One. And then her eyes flew open as Sybil's arm went around her shoulders.

Up close, Sybil studied the damaged face and fought to contain her anger. "Poor child," she said. "Nobody's going to hurt you. Or ask questions, either. Except one. Can you talk?"

There was a space in her head just behind her eyes, and it seemed to be frozen, sealed in so tightly her jaws ached, and her throat. She swallowed once, hard, forced her mouth open. "Yes." It was a whisper, hoarse, as if she'd swallowed sand.

Sybil stepped back. "Good. When you're ready, you can tell us your name and anything you want us to know. And you're welcome to stay here if you want. I'd be glad of the company."

"Stay?" The hoarse whisper came again.

"Why not? You're in no shape to leave."

"You . . . don't . . . know . . . me."

Sybil laid a skirt and blouse on the bed. "All I need to know for now's on your face, child," she said. "You'll stay till we figure what's best to do. Now get dressed and come eat."

Of course, there were good people in the world, she told herself as she struggled to fix her hair. They existed in the pages of the Bible that she'd learned to read herself, slowly, her finger moving beneath the words, her lips silently forming the sounds. Three years of school had given her the basics. She could write, figure numbers, and that, they said, was enough for any girl. She was needed on the farm. She and Beeler who wasn't really her brother but an orphan like she was — adopted off a train and taken away, put to work, ignored for the most part except when they failed to please and got a whipping.

No, she wasn't going back. Might even stay here a while till her face healed, and her arm. Might work for enough wages to buy a ticket to the city. She squared her shoulders inside the blouse that was too large for her but that was clean and smelled faintly of roses. Her mouth twisted in a smile. The clothes she had never smelled of anything but dirt, sweat, sour milk, grease from the stove, and here she was going to a breakfast she hadn't cooked, sitting at the table like a lady instead of a hired hand. She wondered if, after all, she'd be able to eat with them watching, but the growl in her stomach urged her across the room. She opened the door.

Sam was already eating, but at the sight of her, waif-like and lost in his mother's blouse, he got to his feet and pulled out a chair.

"I hope you feel better," he said, sounding foolish to himself.

"Yes. Thank you."

He passed her a blue bowl of eggs, a platter of bacon and potatoes, and on the table were bis-cuits and butter and jam that gleamed red through the sides of a glass jar.

There was so much food! She closed her eyes and said a silent prayer before she began to eat slowly, making it last, while aware of the fact that the man was watching her even as he made easy conversation with his mother. She knew what she looked like. The mirror over the bureau hadn't lied — half her face purple and swollen, her lips bruised, and she wished she looked decent instead of pitiful.

When Sybil got up to clear, she moved to help, wincing as her throbbing shoulder and blistered heels rebelled.

"Sit down, child," Sybil ordered. "You've had a time of it. In a couple days you can help, but not now. And I know I promised not to ask questions, but I can't go on calling you child, so if you have a name, we'd be glad to know it."

"Delia," she said. "My name's Delia." She couldn't bring herself to give the name of her adoptive parents. It wasn't hers, and she wasn't one of them, no matter who said different.

Sybil ignored the omission. "That's pretty, and it suits, too, doesn't it?" She looked at Sam for confirmation, but he was leaning across the table, his dark face serious.

"Is there anybody we should get in touch with?" he asked her. "Family? A friend?"

Her eyes locked on his. "Nobody."

He sat back, irritated with her monosyllabic answers. "Look," he said, "somebody damn near killed you. If I hadn't come along when I did, you'd be lying dead in the ditch, and we can't help you if you don't tell us what happened."

"Sam," Sybil warned.

"I've got to know," he said. "If there's going to be trouble, it's best to be ready."

Delia put her face in her hands. He was right, and she knew it, but she wanted to forget, to pretend she'd just been born without a past, with a clean slate to write on.

Sybil put an arm around her. "Now see," she said to Sam. "You've scared her out of her wits."

"No," Delia said from behind her hands. "He's right. I thought I could do it alone, but I couldn't, after all."

"Do what?" he asked.

She looked up, and once again he was aware of the delicacy of the unmarked half of her face. "Start over," she said. "Lose who they said I was. Delia Persak, an orphan adopted off a train and put to work."

"Ah." Sybil's arm tightened. That explained it. The poor thing had been mistreated, as some of them were, and no way to find out, keep a check on so many children scattered across half the country.

"Best tell us," Sam said, his voice level.

She did. All of it. From the moment she got off the train, an eight-year-old bigger than the rest, and alone with no place to go, no corner in which to hide herself from the pair who took her, who swore to educate her, treat her as their own, like they took the chubby boy called Beeler who pulled her braids and pinched her, and was always in trouble that he brought on himself.

Even she, fresh out of the city, knew the farm where they went was a sorry place, the house a shack, the crops stunted in the field. She'd been glad when they moved across the state where no one knew them, and where she and Beeler worked like animals to keep the four of them alive.

31

There was Beeler, tough and meaner than ever at sixteen, saying: "I'm gettin' out of this rat hole. You can come, too, if you do what I tell you."

But she was frightened, and he ran and was caught. "You squealed, didn't you? Next time I'll break your arm."

But the next time he came after her for a different reason, and she fought him off, terror giving her strength.

"Bitch!"

"I'll tell." Barefoot, she stood in the filthy straw, holding a pitchfork.

"You won't say nothin'. I'll say it was you that asked for it."

And who, after all, would listen? She was only a girl, a stranger in their midst, and one with what they called "bad blood." She had no rights, nor anyone at all to hear.

There had been a woman once, a woman whose face had vanished over the years, but whose words had stayed with her. "Be a good girl, Deely. And I'll come back for you as soon as I can. I promise."

But no one had come — or ever would. She had been sent off on the train with a hundred others, some too young to know what was happening, but all of them rootless, like so many seeds blown by the wind.

She had herself, and her instincts, and a kind of pride that kept her going like a flame that anchored her to earth. So when Beeler caught her again, when he pushed her down into the stones and twisted her arm behind her back, she kicked like a mule, screamed as best she could with her mouth filled with pebbles. And then Pa Persak came, not to save but to accuse.

"A whoor! We've raised us a whoor!" He shouted and rained blows on her face, even though she twisted away.

The woman, his wife, was no better. "Bad blood's what 'tis. She's no better than her ma, even after all we done." She spat a gob of saliva, took Delia by the ear, and tossed her into the root cellar.

They had forgotten to lock the door. Even dazed and beaten, Delia could think rings around them. So she waited, in the dark, and, when they had gone to bed, she pushed open the door, biting her lip at the pain in her shoulder, stepped out, and started walking. She was leaving and never coming back, even if she died. Death, in fact, was better than being beaten and forced to submit like an animal. She walked, she hitched a ride on a farm wagon, hiding under an old canvas, and she walked some more, her vision blurred, her shoulder throbbing, her feet, in the too-small boots, rubbed raw. And then Sam had found her.

There! It was out, all of it. She looked at them, read Sybil's compassion and what seemed to be anger in Sam's eyes. "I won't go back there," she said.

"Certainly not!" That was Sybil.

"You'll stay here," Sam said at last. "And if

33

they trace you, they'll get a taste of their own medicine. How old are you?"

She thought she could like him in spite of that dark face made up of sharp angles.

"Eighteen."

"Then they can't force you."

"I've been told what to do since I can remember," she said, "but no more."

"And none too soon," he said, admiring her flash of courage. Then he pushed back from the table and smiled, and the change in him from darkness to light was startling. "If you ladies will excuse me?"

No one had ever called her a lady. She wanted to laugh and cry at the same time, but all she did was watch him as he opened the door and went out into the gray morning.

Sam had been right when he thought that bringing the girl home would change things. He had stepped into her life and now was responsible for her well-being and even her future, a problem he didn't want, but that had been thrust on him by his own sense of duty.

As she recovered, it seemed to him that no matter where he went, she was there ahead of him — in the kitchen in the morning setting the table, in the orchard where the apple trees were blooming, in the barn or corral asking Will Flanagan a thousand questions, or talking to the mares and new foals, reaching out with her long and graceful arms to stroke a curved neck, touch a curious muzzle. He could hear her voice, faintly hoarse but soothing, like water running over stone, a murmur that ceased when he came near, replaced by an awkward silence as if his presence was somehow disruptive and he had intruded on a private moment.

But dammit! The horses were his, and he had as much right to be there as anyone, especially this slip of a girl who'd come out of nowhere and who danced at the edge of his vision, tantalizing, seen, then not seen, like smoke, like the cranes that came and then flew on, leaving a silence that demanded to be filled.

Who was she? he wondered, then realized that she herself didn't know, that her origins were a mystery and would always be, just as his mother's were.

"Did it bother you?" he asked Sybil, who had come up and was standing beside him, watching the girl and the foals. "Not knowing where you came from or who you were?"

She looked from her son to the girl and back again before she answered. "When I was a child in the orphanage, yes. Not because I wondered about myself, but because I wanted a family of my own, a mother who paid attention just to me. But then I came here, and it was home, and I am who I am because of your grandparents and your father, not because of how or where I was born. Do you see?"

"But what about her?" He gestured at Delia.

Sybil smiled. "She reminds me of me. I was always with the horses, too. Your grandfather thought I was a Gypsy. I think she'll be fine, given a little time."

"Is she staying? I mean we can't just keep her like she's ours. We can't make a hired girl out of her, either, so what's she supposed to do?"

"Like I said, she needs time, and we can give her that. And about doing something, I'm going to teach her to ride. Will says she's half horse, and I believe him. We're going to need a rider for the horse fair, I was thinking."

He blinked, astonished. The horse fair was the event of the year, with buyers coming from as far away as Philadelphia and Boston, and the Gypsies and horse traders who took to the road in summer, busy buying and selling. The climax of the week-long fair was the races, where the Warner horses, ridden by Will's son, Chip, always showed to advantage. Except that Chip had shot up over six feet, and gotten heavy to boot.

"Are you sure you know what you're doing?" he asked, certain she didn't.

"Quite sure." When Sybil spoke like that, there was no getting around it. Besides, he'd never known her to make a bad decision, about business, the horses, or a person's character.

His father would have said — "Have it your way, my dear." — so he said the same, swallowing his doubts.

A month later, watching Delia astride one of the four-year-olds they were taking to the sale, he had to admit that, as usual, Sybil had been right.

Mounted, the self-effacing girl had become a woman, as proud and as confident as a queen. Walk, trot, canter, a creditable side pass down the fence and back, the horse poised and collected under her hand — he saw for himself, but it was still hard to believe.

"How?" he said to Sybil. "How did you do that?"

She chuckled. "She's born for it, bless her. Half horse, like Will said. She asks, the horse gives. It's wonderful."

"You're wonderful," he said. "And so's she, I have to admit."

"Learn to trust your instinct," she said. "I've told you often enough."

He shook his head. "Yours will do. Can she stick at a gallop, do you think?"

"We're working on it. I haven't put her up on Black Warner yet, though."

It was crazy, letting a green girl race, especially on Black Warner, the horse he and his mother had bred. She could show the others in the ring, but to put her out there on twelve hundred pounds of muscle moving at thirty miles an hour was a risk. True, some of the local ranchers put young boys up on their horses for the race, but Delia was a girl and inexperienced.

"What's she have to say about all this?" he asked.

"She doesn't think about anything else. And

she's absolutely fearless."

"She doesn't know any better."

Sybil nodded. "True. But when the time comes, we'll let her make the decision. Like you said, she's not ours."

They were talking about her, Delia knew, and she wanted desperately to please, to receive a word of praise from Sam who so often watched her, and in the watching made her feel that she was misbehaving or acting in a way he felt was inappropriate. She had a memory, very faint, of being held in his arms, and the memory lingered, came back when she least expected it, and always at the wrong time. Like now, with him watching and her blushing like a fool.

The young horse moved restlessly under her, as if sensing her mood, and she wheeled him around and put him into a long trot. Let Sam think what he liked! This motion, this oneness with an animal was enough for her. The joy of it all was sharp in her mouth.

Black Warner pricked his ears and nickered as Delia came into the stable yard. For weeks she had been courting the big horse with apples from the orchard, young carrots from the kitchen garden, with soft words as she groomed his thin-skinned black hide.

"He's a fine horse, miss," Will Flanagan said. "Nervous on the ground, but on his back you can trust him with your life. The missus and me, we've trained him since he was a foal, we have."

Like Sybil and Delia, Will, too, was an orphan, but one who had fought his own way, from the Dublin slums to the back streets of New York, and then West, picking up knowledge of people and horses as he went. And what he thought about Delia was that she had the touch given only to a few, a gift to be used and treasured, like a singing in the heart that never died. Oh, he'd recognized her the first time she'd ventured to the stables, with her eyes wide, her hands stretched out as if she couldn't help herself, and all the horses responding in acknowledgement of one of their own.

He knelt down and cupped his hands. "Up you go, miss. He's a tall one, and no mistake." Like a feather she was, but with strong hands and a steady seat. He stood back, smiling.

"Now what?" she asked.

"Now take him around the pen and get the feel of him. 'Twon't take you long. A mouth like velvet, he has, and you with the sense to feel it."

"Me?" She looked down, eyes bright.

"Aye, miss, and never doubt it."

She leaned toward him over the horse's shoulder. "Will . . . ," her voice faltered. "Will, I don't know who I am. How can I know what I can do?"

She took him aback. How could she not know? "Trust yourself," he said. "Trust what comes, as it will."

Her life whirled in her head — the soft-voiced woman who had called her Deely, the brown

confinement of the orphanage, the terrible swift-
ness of the train, the years of hunger and hos-
tility. And now she was here by a kind of magic,
and on the back of a tall black horse whose heart
beat like a drum under her knees, and whose
body she controlled with a set of reins and a sight
she'd not realized was hers.

"Let's go down the lane," she said.

Will nodded. "I'll be right alongside. For the
first half at least."

She laughed. The sound was merry. "Keep up
now."

"Easier said than done. We'll gallop to the
crossroads and turn back."

She knew the crossroads. It was where she had
turned in her own flight, headed as if by instinct
to this place of refuge. She uttered a quick prayer
of thanks that she was here — secure, blessed,
riding a tall black horse. As she'd been taught,
she warmed him up slowly — a walk, a trot, a slow
canter that was as easy to sit as a rocking chair.

"He's wonderful!"

"And knows it. A proud animal, he is, and
proud to be carryin' a lady."

They reached the top of the lane, and Will settled himself in the saddle. "Now, miss, if you're
ready?"

She nodded.

Black Warner's leap into a gallop took her
breath, nearly unseated her. *Like a tornado,* she
thought when she had her wits back and was
feeling the power of the long stride. Where at

first she had seen this as a game, it became, now, a matter of control, both of herself and of the animal that flowed beneath her. And with that understanding came determination — to succeed, to win, to prove not only her own worth but that of the horse running so powerfully beneath her.

They reached the crossroads, and she turned him, slowly, irrevocably back the way they had come.

Sybil and Sam were waiting, Sam with his heart in his mouth, and Sybil smiling as she watched Delia slow the big horse to a smooth walk.

"How was it?" Sam helped her dismount and, seeing her white face and startled eyes, kept his hands around her waist for fear she was going to faint.

"I never . . . ," she stammered. "I never felt anything so wonderful." She shook her head and walked away from him, and for a moment he saw her as he had the first time — tall, ghostly, her body weaving a spell around itself.

The old trunk lid opened with a puff of dust and a creak of rusty hinges, but the clothes inside were folded neatly and scented with the roses and lavender Sybil gathered in her garden. These were Lucy Warner's clothes, those few that Sybil had never been able to give away or alter — a blue velvet ball gown with matching shoes, a hand-embroidered basque and matching skirt, Sam's christening robe that had been his father's and his father's before him, a hat with a dashing green plume, and, at the bottom, Lucy's black leather boots and riding skirt of fringed buckskin, startling in her day, when most women still rode sidesaddle or drove sedately in buggies and dog-carts.

Lucy had been a tall woman, and slender, and, although Sybil, ever-practical, had cut down many of her dresses, she'd never been able to take the scissors to these. Now she stood, the skirt draped over one arm, the boots in her hand, and called down the hall to Delia who came quickly.

"Ma'am?"

"I want you to try these."

Delia reached out and touched the soft buckskin, then looked up puzzled. "It's beautiful. Whose is it?"

"Yours, if it fits, and I think it will. It was Lucy Warner's a long time ago. She always wore it at the fair and the races, and raised a few eyebrows, I might tell you."

Delia frowned. "I can't," she said.

"Why not?" Heavens, was the girl going to be difficult over a split skirt?

"It's not mine. It belongs to your family."

"Nonsense!" Sybil said. "You remind me of Lucy. And you can hardly go to the races in what you've been wearing. Now try it, and don't fuss so. It's mine to do with as I choose, and, after seeing you this morning, I choose you to have it."

"You've given me so much. I don't know how

to thank you." Delia stood in front of the mirror looking at what she knew was her reflection, but the person gazing back at her was a stranger whom she did not know.

"You just did," Sybil answered, her head cocked. "And like I said, you remind me of Lucy."

Delia turned away from the mirror. "How?"

"Nothing I can put my finger on. Just how you look at times, and when you rode in on Black Warner. Like you'd made up your mind, and that was the end of it."

"We'll win that race for you. I know that much."

"That's what I mean. Lucy couldn't stand losers or losing."

"Who can?"

And that, Sybil thought, disproved any maundering about bad blood or weakness of character. The girl was a winner, and she hoped Sam noticed what a prize he'd brought home.

"That," she said, "is precisely what I meant. Now as long as you're here, I should take your measurements. You'll need a dress. Maybe two." She reached for her sewing basket and tape measure. "It's a good thing bustles are out. They wouldn't have suited you."

"What's a bustle?"

Sybil laughed. "A contraption that stuck out in the back."

"What for?"

"Heaven knows. Somebody thought it was

43

fashionable for women to appear deformed instead of the way God made them."

Delia chuckled in response. "Guess I missed out on that, too. We didn't pay attention to clothes where I came from."

"And that's the first good thing I've heard about it! Now turn around and stand still. I want to get this right the first time."

She was sitting on the bank beside the river that now, in summer, moved slowly, braiding itself around sandbars and small islands, and sending the coolness of water into the warm evening air. The river and its moods fascinated her. She was drawn to it, to its steady flowing, as if it carried within itself the knowledge of a destiny that was both prescribed and unforeseen, a parallel not only with her life but with the lives of all around her.

You were born, she thought, and entered the stream and were carried on it — leaf, twig, small boat — rudderless, at least at first. As a child you had no oars, no understanding of direction. That came with trial, error, struggle, and triumph, however small.

Quietly Sam came out of the brush and sat beside her, and she turned to look at him out of wide-spaced eyes that held the reflection of the river.

"Mind if I sit a while?" he asked.

She had been far away, half hypnotized by water motion and her own formless thoughts, and she struggled to come back to physical reality. "No," she said at last, nothing more, and they sat in silence a while, each wondering what to say or whether to speak at all.

Finally, unable to stand the quiet, she said: "Did you want something?"

The question irritated him. Did he have to want anything more than to sit here enjoying the peace and the sight of her in her blue dress, dreaming whatever it was that she dreamed?

"No," he said. Then — "Yes." — and stopped, attempting to put his worries into words.

"What?" Her eyebrows were half moons, raised delicately.

"It's this business of you racing Black Warner. If my mother's put you up to it, I want to know, because you don't have to do it if you don't want."

"But I do," she said.

"It's dangerous."

"I'm not afraid."

"Then you're crazy. It's a rough game, and you could get killed. Think about that." He watched her and saw frown lines gather between her eyes.

"It's people that scare me," she said. "Not horses, and not Black Warner. It's people that nearly killed me." Then, seeing him frown in return, she smiled. "I'll be fine. Really. You don't have to worry about me."

"I do, though." He knew it was true. The thought of her lifeless under the hoofs of horses was a nightmare.

"Nobody ever worried about me before. I don't know how to take it." She looked down at her hands that were clasped in her lap, thinking that now, in return, she would have to worry about him because that was what happened when you were close enough to someone to know what they felt.

"It's all right to change your mind," he said. "If you do, tell me."

"I won't change it." Riding that race was proof of herself. She couldn't give in simply because he was troubled.

Sam sighed. She was stubborn, but, more than that, she was courageous and tough, a far cry from the limp creature he'd carried home three months before.

A few fireflies were drifting through the brush, blinking on and off, signaling each other. He watched them a minute, seeing himself as a kid, catching hundreds of the little insects and sealing them in one of his mother's canning jars.

"Did you ever chase them when you were little?" he asked. "I did. I'd take the jar to bed with me and watch them till I fell asleep."

"I wasn't ever that little."

The truth of the statement, the bleakness of her lost childhood caught him unaware. He wanted to reach out and hold her, but, if he did, she might disappear in that way she had, leaving him with only the swirl of his emotions.

"I wish. . . ." He shook his head.

"What?" Again the raising of eyebrows.

"It wasn't fair, what happened to you."

"It's done now." She looked away from him, across the river. "It's finished."

"What if it isn't? Have you thought they might be at the fair? Your pa and brother?"

The color drained out of her face, and her hands clenched. Then she relaxed. "They never went before. Least, not that I knew. And, besides, Pa couldn't afford any of those horses."

He leaned toward her. "Keep it in mind just in case. And if you see them, tell me. Promise." He reached out and took her hand, felt the strength in the long fingers, in the palm callused from years of hard work. "Will you promise?"

If she did, there would be a fight, a dirty one, Pa and Beeler against Sam, no rules, nothing but brutality, animals striking out at each other.

"I don't want you hurt," she said, refusing to answer.

"Why not?"

"I just don't." She stood up abruptly, shook out her skirt, and tossed her braid behind her. "We'd best get back, it's getting dark."

On the way up the hill, she put out her hands and captured a firefly. Its light came through her fingers, a strange, yellow-white luminescence, proof of a life that could be snuffed out in an instant. With that, she opened her hand and let the insect fly, and watched until it disappeared into the thick grass.

She made a picture standing there in the blue twilight, skirt blowing around her ankles, her head raised in something that looked to Sam like wonder. He wished he could keep the moment, could keep her as she was, fire, air, water all combined into one body. He wished he were a poet or a painter, or anyone at all except who he was — a good man who had no words.

It was years since Delia had been in a town. As soon as she had shown signs of becoming a woman and attractive, the Persaks had left her at home when they went on their infrequent shopping trips, knowing she was too valuable to lose to some neighboring farmer who was taken by a pretty face.

Awed by the crowds, the noise, she stood on the sidewalk and stared. Flags waved, bunting was hung on the storefronts, farm wives and the wives of the town's businessmen were all out dressed in their best, and down the middle of the street came a Gypsy caravan, gaily painted and pulled by four flashy paint horses.

"Oh, look at them!" she exclaimed to Sybil.

"Pretty. And probably wild as March hares," came the reply. "But the Gypsies have some fine animals, as you'll see for yourself."

Delia's head kept swiveling. "This is a real city!" she said.

"It's getting there. It's three times as big as it was when I first saw it. Back then it was pretty sorry looking, but, even so, I was scared to death."

"I guess we all were," Delia said. "There was a

boy on my train, just a little thing. He cried all the way from New York. I often wonder what happened to him."

"He might've been lucky. Some of us were."

Delia smiled. "I'm lucky now. But I never was in a hotel before. Is there anything I need to do?"

Sybil took her arm and walked her into the lobby. "Just be yourself. We're sharing a room, so you won't be alone, and Sam will be here to take us to supper."

That was another thing. She'd never eaten anywhere but at home. On horseback she felt secure, but in this place everything seemed an obstacle to be gotten around. She wished she were camped out with Will, Chip, and the horses, with no need to worry she'd make a mistake and shame Sybil and Sam.

"I shouldn't have come," she said.

"Nonsense! Besides, you didn't expect to spend your life hidden away, did you?"

"I never thought." And that was the trouble. She'd just floated along like that rudderless boat she'd seen so clearly.

At least, thanks to Sybil, she had a new dress to wear, and Lucy's riding skirt and boots. At least she wouldn't disgrace Sam and Sybil by her clothes, even if she didn't know how to act in hotels and fancy restaurants.

She sighed. "There's so much to learn."

"And there are those who don't know as much as you do. Think of it that way," Sybil advised, and took her arm. "Come on now. Let's go and unpack our clothes and then we'll go out and see how Will and Chip are doing with the horses."

There were so many people! After five days of showing the horses and being introduced as a family friend, Delia found she was longing for the quiet of the ranch — the pleasant and unhurried meals, the long twilights, the uninterrupted silence of the land that in itself was a subtle voice.

"I'm going to walk out to camp and see Black Warner," she said after supper.

Sam folded his napkin and put it on the table. "I'll go with you."

"You don't have to."

"I want to. I've had enough of town to last me."

So he didn't want her company! Well, she didn't need his, either. She stood up. "Let's go then."

Looking after them, Sybil let out her breath in a hiss, wondering when they would stop acting like strangers with each other. Both of them stubborn, she decided, and used to keeping to themselves. Even as a child, Sam had fought his own battles, refusing help, never asking advice, but her feeling about Delia remained strong, and she wanted it made visible. Over and above that, she wanted the two of them to know and share in her own happiness. She wanted her life and the life she had spent with Jake to go on, proof of goodness, a bulwark against the evils of the world, those people who, like the Persaks, had ravaged the children placed in their care.

"Damnation!" She rarely swore, but it felt good so she repeated herself. "Damnation!"

"I'll be glad when it's over, and we can go home."

They were walking up the hill toward the horse camp, the fires of the summer traders lighting the way. "So many people! I can't even remember their names."

Sam noticed her use of the word home. "I'm glad you know you've got a home," he said. "So's my mother. It's been nicer since you came."

Pleased at the compliment, she stopped walking. "I figured I was a nuisance sometimes. Like I did things wrong and made you mad."

What she'd done was turn him as awkward as an adolescent, and he was damned tired of it. "It's that way you have of disappearing," he said to her. "Even when you're right in front of my eyes. I thought you were a ghost that night I found you, and there's times I still think I'm seeing things, or that you're avoiding me. That's what gets me, not you exactly."

She laughed then, the shadow that had been in her eyes gone. "I'm real enough," she said.

A stick snapped somewhere in the woods behind them, and Sam heard the faint rustling of leaves. He took her arm. "Let's get up to camp."

She had heard, too. "What is it?"

"Might be nothing. Might be a person. And us

standing out here like targets."

She gripped his arm hard. "You don't think it's them! It can't be. I've been looking all week like you said to."

"Hard to find anybody in the crowd. Come on." He pulled her up the path past the Gypsy camp where the paint horses were tied.

"There they are, those pretty critters," she said, distracted, and the tall man standing beside the caravan turned.

"Any one would make a nice horse for a lady. Especially a lady who rides like you." He showed white teeth in a smile.

Delia had seen him watching her as she showed a horse to a buyer. Now the compliment and the expression on Sam's face made her want to giggle, in spite of what might be in the woods. "I don't need a horse," she told him. "But thank you for the kind words."

He bowed, then looked past them down the trail. "Why are you running?"

"Can't be too careful," Sam said. "I heard something back there."

"You don't carry money?" It seemed a casual question, but Sam stiffened.

"My money's safe in the bank."

"Ah," said the Gypsy before turning back to Delia. "Then guard your woman. She's worth much more than gold."

She felt her neck prickle. What did he know? Everybody said Gypsies could tell the future. She tugged on Sam's arm. "Let's go." And to the

Gypsy: "Thanks again."

"Remember what I say." He walked back to the caravan, a dark figure against the glow of the fire.

In his twenty-six years, Sam had never had reason to be jealous of anyone, so he was unprepared for the force of the emotion when it came. He could foresee every eligible male in the state coming to the house hoping to possess what he had taken for granted. Delia. His Delia.

Within sight of Will's fire he stopped and pulled her to face him. "Marry me," he said.

She had been thinking of the Gypsy's warning, had been back on the hard-scrabble farm with Beeler lusting after her, and Sam's words went through her like a knife. When she answered, she watched his face with wide eyes. "Do you mean it?"

"Yes. Damn it, Deely. It's the truth. You heard what he said. He said . . . 'your woman' . . . and that's what you are. Since that first day it's been you, only I didn't see right off."

But she had learned things in the last months. She said: "I'm not anybody's woman but my own." And then hoped to God she hadn't made a mistake.

He stepped back as if she'd hit him. "What's got into you? I want to marry you. Keep you safe. Spend my life with you. We fit, you and me, even if you do go off into your head sometimes."

She stood, folding her arms under her breasts, and the light of the rising moon struck sparks from her hair. "I don't know much about marriage," she said slowly. "Only what your mother's told me. But she and your father loved each other, and it wasn't about who belonged to who, or who had peculiar habits. Do you love me, Sam? As I am? Or is it something else?"

In all his life Sam had never had to define the term. He'd only seen love in action, been the recipient of his parents' caring. Forced to look inward, he found a barren place, and a wild crying like the music of the cranes, a song that had no words, only the longing — *his* — for this woman he had, by chance, brought to life, and who could slip through his fingers as easily as rain.

He took her face in his hands, smoothed the slightly crooked cheek bone with his thumb. "I want you to be with me," he said. "Every day and every night. Love's just a word. What's inside's different. What's inside is like a singing. Can you hear it, Deely?"

She thought she could. And she thought she'd never dreamed such sweet words, even when she'd dared to dream, even when she dreamed about the woman who once had called her Deely. Slowly her lips curved in a smile. "I never heard anybody say anything so pretty. Or heard music like that, either."

He saw in an instant what life would be like without her — a sameness, a solitude, a yearning never fulfilled. "Does that mean you will?" he asked, and looked away from her lest he see what he dreaded in her eyes. He was stunned when she moved against him, put her head on his shoulder.

"I will." It was a whisper.

Neither of them heard the footsteps or saw the watcher, his face distorted by rage and by the moving shadows of the leaves.

"When you win, I want you to keep the prize money." Sybil was sitting on the bed, watching Delia pull on her boots.

"But I can't!" She looked up, startled.

"Every wife needs a little pocket money to use as she pleases."

"But. . . ."

Sybil shook her head. "False pride leads nowhere. You and Sam have made me happy. If you don't know what to do with the money, put it in the bank."

"I've never even been inside a bank."

Sybil smiled. "You've never been married before, either."

"And you make everything sound so easy. It scares me. Nothing's ever been easy for me, you understand. So how can I trust all of this?"

"You take it a day at a time. Faith in life isn't given, but it does come if you let it."

Delia stomped her foot into the boot, walked over to the older woman, and knelt beside her. "I wish I'd known you first," she whispered. "It all would've been different."

Sybil reached out and smoothed the dark hair. "But you're here now. That's what's important."

She stood and pulled Delia with her. "Now we'd better hurry. Black Warner doesn't like to stand around on race day."

They drove to the horse camp in the buggy, Sybil waving and returning the greetings of friends and well-wishers with obvious pleasure. Nothing could dim her happiness this day. She had no doubt that Delia and Black Warner would win, and then they could go home and make plans for the wedding.

She wished Jake were there to share in the excitement and give his blessing to the match. It was times like this when she missed him most, the boy, and the man he'd become. She clasped her hands tightly in her lap. Happiness, after all, was fleeting.

Beside her, Delia was silent, going over the race course, attempting to focus on what lay ahead, but unable to take her eyes off Sam, whose face, under the dark hat brim, was serious.

"Don't take any chances," he told her. "This won't be like riding down the lane. There'll be a bunch of untrained kids on horses running wild. Keep out of their way if you can. Winning isn't everything."

Yes it is. Delia set her chin. And yet, it was wonderful to be fussed over, the object of his concern. She wanted to dance and sing, celebrating her own joy. Instead, she leaned close to him and put a hand on his arm.

"We'll be fine. I promise you."

"I couldn't stand to lose you," he said. "Not now."

Her laughter was sweet. "You won't. Not now. Not ever."

At the camp, Will was walking an excited Black Warner, doing his best to calm the animal. "He knows," he said. "And he's ready."

The big horse blew and danced sideways, then settled as Delia stroked the shining curve of his neck, but, once in the saddle, she felt the fire inside him, a wildness that was hers to control, and she forgot everything but the responsibility before her and the lessons she had so eagerly learned.

"I'll ride him down through the woods," she said to Sam. "Meet you at the track."

"Deely. . . ."

"Hush!" It was an order. Then her mouth curved in a smile. "I love you. But today it's Black Warner's turn." She wheeled and rode off down the narrow trail.

Black Warner wanted to run, to race against himself, kept testing the bit, asking permission, and she spoke softly, holding him in. "Not yet. Not now. Just go easy, easy, easy." It was a tuneless song, soothing, pacifying, and the horse cocked one ear back to listen, while the other stayed alert, pricked forward, seeking an excuse to disobey.

She kept him to a jog that was like a dance, his big hoofs almost soundless on the moist forest floor, and they rounded the last curve of the trail, pleased with one another.

With no warning, two men darted out, one leaping for Black Warner's head, the other clawing at her leg, firm in the stirrup.

"Who . . . ?" She raised her crop and brought it down across the man's face, saw the stripe of blood, at the same moment she recognized Pa Persak.

The sound that came from her throat matched the squeal of the horse, high and guttural, a battle cry. Again she gripped Black Warner with her knees as he dropped back on powerful haunches, then reared and struck at the boy's head. Then, with a leap, he moved into a run.

"Oh, God," she whimpered. "Oh, God." And clung to the dark mane, to the saddle, to what was left of her wits as they thundered down the trail and onto the race grounds.

Somehow she pulled him in, came to a sliding stop, and looked around wildly for Sam.

"Deely! What? What happened?" He was at her side, fear and anxiety distorting his face.

"It was them. Pa. And . . . and Beeler. In the woods." She clamped her jaws together to keep her teeth from chattering.

"Are you hurt?"

She shook her head.

"Where are they now?"

Behind closed lids, she saw it all again — the old man and the blood on his face, in his beard, and Beeler, his mouth open in terror as the horse struck him down.

"Beeler's dead," she whispered.

A crowd had gathered around them. She caught a glimpse of the Gypsy, his eyes somber.

Sam controlled his anger. How dare they frighten her, bring that look of desperation to her eyes? "Stay here. I'll get the sheriff, and we'll see about this."

"Past the bend. Black Warner reared. I. . . . I couldn't hold him." What was it Will had said early on — that she could trust the horse with her life? Well, she had. She leaned down and stroked his neck that was glistening with sweat. "He saved me. It wasn't his fault. They jumped out at us without warning."

"Get down and come in the shade. Let the men handle this." Sybil stood beside her, worried.

If she got down, she knew her legs would give out. "I'm all right."

"Of course, you are. But you've had a shock."

"She kilt him! She kilt my boy!" The scream was ragged, but loud enough so that everyone turned to see an apparition staggering down the hill.

"She's the devil's own! Her and that black beast!" Blood was dripping into his beard and spattering his shirt that was open and flapping around his knees.

Sam dropped Black Warner's bridle and stepped out to intercept the old man, and, as he did, the horse's ears went back flat against his head. He struck the ground hard with one great hoof and snorted a challenge, and Delia, feeling his fury rising, gathered the reins and held him still.

"He is your defender." The Gypsy reached out for the bridle. "A horse like this is worth a thousand others."

"He hates to be stopped," she admitted. "They . . . that old man and the boy jumped out at us."

"And got what they deserved. Both of them fools to try such a thing."

"Worse than that," she said.

"There's nothing worse than a fool. See him!" He gestured at Persak who was babbling at Sam and the sheriff. "What is he if not a fool and, because of that, evil?"

Evil. The truth sank into her. He was evil, this wild-eyed creature, and the rebellious boy, the old woman with her snuff-blackened teeth. Unconsciously her fingers tightened around her whip, and Black Warner, reading her intention, threw up his head.

But the Gypsy was quick. "No more," he said. "Enough."

As if he felt their attention, Persak turned, pointed a gnarled finger at Delia.

"There she is! The whoor. The devil's daughter."

Sam's punch to his jaw happened so quickly, no one, afterward, could say they'd seen it, only seen the old man on the ground and Sam standing over him, fists clenched.

"She is going to be my wife," he snarled. "The girl you beat and starved and tried to kidnap. And by God, old man, I'll kill you if you say another word!"

Ryerson, the sheriff, reached down and hauled Persak to his feet. "Let's go."

"I raised her up from nothing!" Persak protested. "See how I've been repaid!"

"Shut up."

But the old man wrestled himself to a stop beside Delia and stared at her. "You'll burn," he hissed at her. "You'll burn in hell."

"The wicked burn," she said, her voice carrying clearly. "The people like you who took a child and tried to turn her into an animal."

She glanced around, recognized faces in the crowd — traders, buyers, neighbors recently met, women who, like her, were destined to be wives, mothers, and responsible for the lives of those around them. And she saw herself as she had been, frightened but hopeful, innocent of the horrors that awaited.

Swallowing hard, she went on, weaving the tapestry of her life and gaining confidence with every sentence. "I was an orphan. Adopted by this man and his wife, abused by them in ways none of you could believe. And the orphan trains are still running. They're full of babies and children who deserve a chance. My misfortune was this man and his wife, but I escaped, maybe just so I could tell what happened to me and might be happening around you. So I could beg your kindness for those children as well as your own."

Around her the crowd was silent, listening. She lifted her head. "I am not a whore. If I was, I wouldn't be here, engaged to be married. In a few months I'll be Delia Warner. Until then, I don't have a name, because never, while I live, will I be called by the name of this man."

"Good for you, gal!" someone shouted.

"Let's get the old bugger!"

"Hang the son-of-a-bitch!"

Without warning, the crowd turned mob and surged toward Persak who was writhing like an insect in the sheriff's grip.

"Stop it! Stop it right now!" Delia wheeled Black Warner and shouted over the top of the mob, her voice like a blast from a trumpet.

"He's not worth killing. Not worth having on your consciences." Satisfied that they were inclined to listen, she smiled, her blazing crooked smile, and raised her whip high. "This is race day! Have you forgot? We've got a race to run, so let's do it!"

"That's one fine woman," the sheriff said to Sam. "As for this . . . this critter, I'll throw him in jail and let him think it over. He'll be there, if you want to press charges."

Persak's lip raised in a snarl. "She kilt my boy. I'm the one who's pressing charges."

"Shut up, you." Ryerson shook him hard. "I'm the sheriff here, not you, and there's laws about accosting women and beating little kids."

"Beeler!"

"I'll see he gets buried. Now move."

Sam said nothing. The fierce woman he'd just seen in action bore no trace of the ragged girl he'd brought home — or maybe she did. Maybe that ferocity was what had kept her going, refused to let her die. And she was his!

He walked over to her, put a hand on her knee. "You don't have to race. You've been through enough, don't you think?"

She leaned down and touched his head, a caress. "If I don't, Black Warner will never forgive me. Worse, *I* won't forgive me. Now wish me luck and go sit with your mother by the finish."

He didn't want her to go. He wanted to say that winning wasn't important. But he found himself wordless, as so often was the case, yet with music stirring inside — cymbals, fiddles, flutes — a harmony he finally understood.

"Go on, then," he said. "Go on, and God bless."

At the starting line she glanced quickly at the other entries. The Gypsy was beside her on a dish-faced, sleek gray mare she hadn't seen before. Clever of him, she thought, to keep her hidden, the one Black Warner would have to beat.

"Good luck to you, lady."

"And to you."

He thought perhaps she was Rom — one of his people — abandoned, left for strangers to care

63

for. A pity. She would have made a fine wife, bear many sons. As it was, she and the horse made good rivals, both fiery-eyed and courageous. And then he had no more time to wonder or admire, as the ten horses leaped into a gallop, and his mare, bred for endurance, settled into her steady stride.

There was noise — the sound of pounding hoofs, of wind in her ears, the creak of saddles, the hard breathing of straining horses — and beneath her Black Warner's increasing determination, a heated arrogance, a fury to out-distance the rest. One by one he left them behind, left all in his dust but the gray mare, more bird than horse, her high-set tail like a taunt. *Catch me! Catch me!*

They rounded the turn almost in tandem, and the last mile stretched ahead, too long, too short, Delia thought, unaware that she thought at all.

And then it happened, what she could never later describe, only liken to an explosion, as Black Warner reached into the depths of himself, into his Thoroughbred heart, and with ears flat, great neck stretched out, caught his rival, passed her, and kept on, his speed so great that Delia's eyes blurred. She could not see, and didn't have to, knowing by the cheers that she and the horse had won.

"Enough!" Sybil fanned herself with her hand. "Any more days like this will be the end of me!"

"You love it all," Sam said.

"Well . . . yes," she agreed. "But I'm ready for a nap, a good dinner, and home tomorrow."

"Me, too." Delia sat beside her on the buggy seat, worn out but still hearing the cheers of the crowd, feeling the stunning motion of Black Warner as he crossed the finish line.

"Home." She closed her eyes and saw the place where she had been allowed to become herself, where no one had condemned her but only offered encouragement.

"Lady." The Gypsy stood, the reins of the gray mare loose in his hand, and she went to him, half ashamed that she and Black Warner had beat him and the lovely creature whose head was still high and whose nostrils showed crimson.

"A good race."

He nodded, smiled a smile that encompassed them all. "And a fair one." He searched her face with dark eyes and then went on. "A wedding gift for you and your husband." He put the mare's reins in her hand. "May you have fine horses and a happy life."

Delia stepped back. "I can't," she said. "I can't take her. It isn't right."

"It isn't right to refuse."

Puzzled, she looked at him who seemed to be speaking only to her.

"Then, thank you. She's beautiful and . . . and wonderful. I'll care for her always." Still she was puzzled, feeling a link between this man and herself, a calling from a place she couldn't fathom, an echo as if, overhead, the cranes were speaking

65

in a multitude of voices the way she'd heard them on the lane.

"If ever you or your people need a place to rest, please come to us," she told him. "You'll always be welcome."

Sybil slipped down from the wagon and linked her arm through Delia's. "Always," she agreed.

He took their hands, bowed over them. "I wish you all good things. Long life and happiness," he said, and then was gone.

Delia looked at the mare, at Black Warner, at Sybil and Sam.

"Let's all of us go home," she said.

Loner

The wind came out of the north long and low and level, and with it came snow, lightly at first, then heavier, blotting out the rise and fall of the plains, making the earth indistinguishable from sky.

Lyle sank his chin into the collar of his coat, pulled his hat low over his eyes. May in Montana! In Texas the bluebonnets would be out, the flycatchers buzzing, the rivers running fast and full, colored red like the dirt that contained them. Here there was only earth and sky, and the mouth of the wind that sought to swallow him.

Maybe he'd been foolish to agree to this venture, even if cattlemen were flocking to Montana, lured by the prospects of land for the taking, free graze and good water, even if, after all these years, something in him he hadn't wanted to recognize kept urging him to stop moving, to leave a mark that said he'd been more than simply a man quick with a gun, deft with a deck of cards.

He'd been brought up to know better, except all that early training had been of no use to him at all with his family lying slaughtered like so many sheep, their blood soaking into the ground, and him standing there swearing a man's vengeance.

At times like this he felt cut in half, with a curtain pulled down between the boy and the man, a curtain that denied him feeling and bred caution, that had made him what he was — a man without fear or any emotion he could name. Yet here he was, headed for a second chance, and in a country cold enough to freeze the ears off a mule.

He'd come on ahead of Sam and the boys who were driving the cattle simply because he'd wanted to be alone, to stake his own claim on the place and learn it without advice or intrusion.

He and Sam had come up the fall before to look over the country — the rolling plains, naked except for a blanket of curling buffalo grass, the river and the creek that flowed to the Yellowstone with its breaks and lush stands of bluejoint, and always, west and south, the horizon defined by mountains, invisible now as if they'd been blown away by the wind and the driving snow.

Somewhere up ahead was the home place and a cabin. Somewhere. . . .

"Best stay put a while," the bartender in the last town, an old prize fighter whose nose was too mushed to support his spectacles, had warned that morning. Or had it been the morning before? Time out here had a way of slipping past, one day into another, the red dawn erupting into the volcanic purple and gold of sunset, obliterating the miles traveled as if they'd never been.

The bartender wore a skullcap of tightly woven wool that had a string attached to the bridge of his spectacles, giving him an appearance halfway between a badger and a bulldog, and his eyes glinted like pebbles behind the thick lenses. "A spring blizzard's just as bad as a winter one," he'd said. "Mark me."

Impatient, Lyle had ignored the advice and headed out into the grayness of morning, across the rise and fall of the naked plains, with here and there a snowdrift like a white shadow on brown earth, and all the while the wind coming stronger, with an edge to it that warned of worse to come.

His big roan raised its head, snorted, blew steam out of ice-crusted nostrils. It was a good horse, steady, muscled, broad-chested — worth the ninety-five dollars he'd paid in Miles City, with the pack horse thrown in. Glancing back, he saw that it, too, was staring off into the whiteness through eyelashes coated with a heavy fringe of ice.

On the back of the wind came the faint blue scent of woodsmoke, and, like the horses, Lyle lifted his head. Smoke meant people, and he wasn't in a position to be particular about what kind of people — buffalo hunters, trappers, maybe just a bunch of out-of-work cowhands holed up for the winter in a line shack. What the hell? The numbness in his fingers and toes was a warning, like the steady snow screen that made a mockery of a man's sense of direction.

He wasn't about to die out here, wasn't about to let his life get buried in a drift, although maybe that was all he deserved. Maybe. He urged the roan on, following the smoke that laid a trail of warmth, beckoned like a mirage seen at a distance. Even so, he nearly missed the cabin, half dug-out, half logs that sprouted out of the side of a hill, would have gone on past except for the roan that stopped dead, nickered, and was answered by a faint whinny.

Then he saw the pale light, like a will-o'-the-wisp, seen, then not seen, moving slowly away. "Hello the house!" he called, and the wind took his voice, sent it off in fragments.

The light swung once, then stopped, and he called again, riding toward it through drifts up to the roan's belly.

"Stop right there." The shotgun was aimed at his mid-section, and the woman holding it had the yellow eyes of a lynx, unblinking, unreadable.

Automatically he lifted his hands. "Sorry to frighten you, ma'am."

The gun didn't waver. "What do you want?"

What in hell did she think he wanted on a night like this? He choked down the question. "I was hoping I could put up till the snow stops. Your shed'd do me."

She came a step closer, and he saw she was tall, and good to look at in spite of those eyes that were narrowed now, squinting up at him.

"Get out." The two words came like the spit of a cat. "You and your kind aren't welcome here."

She meant it. She'd turn him away, drill a hole through him without any hesitation if he was any judge, and he was. What did she mean: your kind?

"Just what kind am I?" he said, failing to keep the beginnings of anger out of his voice.

She gave a snort. "Just git. You whisky peddlers have caused enough damn' trouble."

The roan shifted under him, restless, turning toward the shelter of the barn, and the anger that was always there danced under Lyle's skin. Cautiously he swung down and stood facing her, knowing he could take the shotgun away in one quick move, knock her down in the snow. But he'd never hit a woman and didn't intend to start now.

"I'm no whisky trader. Me and my partner filed on a place north of here, but I'm not going to make it tonight."

She stared at him. "Just what we need. More homesteaders turning the grass upside down."

Probably deliberately she'd misunderstood, intended to stand here trading insults until they both turned to ice.

"It beats whisky peddling."

"Not by much." She gestured with the shotgun. "All right. Put up in the shed. I don't want a neighbor on my conscience. But you better not be lying. And stay away from the mare.

She's ready to foal."

His mouth quirked in a smile. Just like a female to choose the worst possible time. But what was this woman doing out here alone, no husband in evidence? She had a long braid of yellow hair that came down over her shoulder — a thick braid, big around as his wrist and turning white with snow.

"You'd best get inside," he said. "I'll be fine in the shed. And if it'll make you feel any better, my name's Lyle Speaks. I'll be running cattle and horses, and that's all."

She stared at him as if she were memorizing his face or trying to see behind it. Then she said, with the smallest hint of humor: "It beats homesteading."

"Yes, ma'am." He picked up his reins.

"My name's Clytie Beck," she said.

He liked the sound of it — hard and soft together — wondered if she wasn't like her name, soft under the shell she wore like a turtle, like the oversize buffalo coat that hid all but her face.

"A pleasure," he said, tasting the irony of it — the two of them at odds, him banished to a barn when in the house there was a fire and warmth, escape from the wolf howl of storm, and the woman, brittle, yellow-eyed, guarding her door.

The barn was as tidy as a kitchen, bridles on wall pegs, worn saddles beneath, hay stacked where the horses couldn't get at it. There were two of them, both mares, both several cuts above the usual range horses and well cared for. They watched him with bright, intelligent eyes as he unsaddled, and again he wondered what the woman was doing here, so obviously alone and used to it.

"And you won't tell me," he said to the mares. "You're all in it together." He saw nothing strange in his one-sided conversation, a habit with him as with most riders — talking to his horses and to himself.

He rubbed down his own animals, then threw each a good forkful of the sweet-scented hay. It was good hay, the perfume bringing back memories he'd tried to block. The long light of summer evenings and the music of womens' voices — his mother's and Beth's, and himself a boy again, trusting, innocent of the future.

It had been a long road from Texas to here, and nothing to show for it but ugliness. He'd never thought to harm a living thing until that day, but after that he hadn't cared, not for himself or anyone else, and now he was here, the future unknown, the night ahead full of storm and the moan of wind around the corners of the barn.

One of the mares pawed the straw with a powerful hoof, turned around, then lay down with a grunt. Her time, regardless of weather, and would the woman, Clytie, want to know, to be here instead of safe behind her barred door? He knew the answer, just as he knew what he was doing was an excuse to go out across the yard, bent against the wind, toward the dug-out and Clytie with amber eyes the color of lantern light.

"Now what?" She stood peering at him through a crack in the door. Prickly she was in spite of their being neighbors.

Behind her he glimpsed a fire where a pot hung cooking, tempting, fragrant. "Your mare's foaling. I thought you'd want to know." He resisted the urge to push the door open.

"I'll be right there." The door closed, and he was standing like a god-damned beggar on the step, like a homeless pup, a god-damned fool.

"Bitch!" The word came out sharp, and he turned on his heel and went back to the barn, ignoring his hunger aroused by the scent of the stew, and another, subtler wanting he had no intention of satisfying. He'd never begged in his life, never had to, and, if the rest of his neighbors were like her, he'd be out of here and back in Texas before spring.

She pushed open the barn door, her lantern held high. "How is she?"

"Fine. So far." He'd be damned if he'd give her an inch. "Is this her first?"

Clytie shook her head. "No. She's a good mother. I . . . we've had her a while."

He noted the substitution and how she'd smothered her words, but he made no response. In his life he'd always waited to see how the wind blew, to estimate the position of whomever he was facing. It had always paid off.

"Shouldn't be too long now," was all he said as he hunkered down at the entrance to the stall. "But it's a good thing she's in here. It's no night for a foal to be out in."

Clytie hung the lantern on a peg, and he saw the set of her chin and something that looked like desperation in her eyes.

"I can't afford to lose any more stock," she said. "You'll find out how it is, and then you'll understand why I didn't want you here."

"Tell me."

She knelt down and stroked the mare's neck, an oddly gentle gesture, unlike the woman she'd seemed, and again he was curious at what appeared to be contradictions in her — hard and soft, jagged and smooth — so a man didn't know where he stood. When she spoke, her voice was rough, as if she was swallowing tears.

"We've got rustlers, Indians, whisky traders, nothing but trouble. The traders sell their rotgut to the Indians. It's illegal, but they're smart and greedy. They take horses as payment, run them into the badlands, change the brands, then sell them in Canada. They don't care how many horses the Indians steal to pay for their damned whisky, or who they steal from. They don't care about dead cattle or dead ranchers, either. All they know is that they're getting rich off the rest of us, and we're helpless." She sat back on her heels, her hands clutched in her lap.

"The Indians in Canada come down here, get drunk, rob and kill, and then go back, and the

British don't do anything about it. Our own agents won't do anything about the Montana Indians, and the damned soldiers at the forts just sit there watching us honest folks go broke. You'll find out, Mister Speaks. You'll find out when your cattle are dead and the Indians blame you because they're hungry and they say that you, all by yourself, killed off the buffalo. And when your horses disappear and nobody will lift a finger to help. I've lost half my herd and can't afford any more. It's a sorry state when you can't trust a person. When what you've sweated for gets taken, and you're back where you started with nothing left but the back end of a dream."

He listened carefully, making note of the fact that once again she referred only to herself, but when he spoke, he ignored the fact.

"What about our Indians? Seems to me they can be kept in line."

She snorted. "They're worse than anybody . . . stealing, going on drunk rampages, and the agents support them. You need their permission to get on the reservation, even to look for your own property, and they won't give it. Every damn' one of 'em's a gentleman from the East, hand-picked not to cause trouble, to protect the red man, and, incidentally, to line their own pockets, and they don't give a hoot about us ranchers getting back what's ours." She emphasized the *gentleman,* making it sound like a cuss word.

Trouble. Wherever he went. And Montana

wasn't going to be any different. One thing he knew, no Indian was about to take what was his. Never again. He said: "Sounds like you folks need a little help."

Her laugh was brittle. "You're welcome to try. The government just ignores us, like we're at the root of the problem."

"And your husband?" He took her off guard, watched her hands clench tighter, so he could see the white knobs of bone, the curiously small wrists that stuck out from the ragged cuffs.

"He's dead. A year now. He went out after our horses and never came back." The yellow eyes were once again without expression — secretive, flat, hiding an emotion too dreadful to be exposed. "The Indians got him. I found him when the snow melted. Buried what was left."

He was back again in Texas, the boy propelled into manhood, seeing the mangled bodies, the grimaces of death. With one sentence she'd managed to rip aside the curtain he'd kept closed, the veil between himself and the memory too agonizing to be born. See it again and go berserk, remember and puke until there was nothing left but the hatred. There was always hate. It kept him going, fueled the reason for what he was.

He said: "Comanches massacred my family. I'm all that's left."

Her expression didn't change. "When?"

"I was thirteen."

"God-damn the varmints. God-damn them to hell."

"Living is hell," he said, knowing the truth of it.

"The trouble is, dying's worse. I've seen enough of it to know. And when you're left, you wonder why."

"I knew why."

She looked at him with that curious way she had of seeing under his bones, and nodded once. "You got them," she said. "Then you found out you couldn't stop. Am I right?"

"That's how it was."

"I'd do it, too, but I'm a woman. It's hard for a woman, even though the need is there."

"It doesn't get easier," he said. "Man or woman."

Her hands lay loose in her lap, as if she'd expended all her energy reliving tragedies hidden away but not forgotten. "Reckon that's so," she said softly. "And I'm sorry for it. For you and me."

"It's done now."

She shook her head. "Things like that, they stay with you. Mark you. I know, and I wish I didn't. Sometimes at night I see him . . . what there was after the wolves got done, and it's like it's happening all over, like I'm digging the grave and putting him in it. Mostly bones, you know, not the man I knew."

He said: "They even killed our chickens. Wrung their necks and let them lie where they fell."

"It makes you wonder, doesn't it? We're taught

that killing is wrong, but sometimes it's what you have to do to make something right."

"There's folks who'd argue that."

She looked up at him, her mouth twisted. "There's folks who can't tell what direction they're going even with a signpost."

Beside them the mare grunted, arched her back, and grunted again, and then the foal slid out, shining in its sack, and lay still, a butterfly wrapped in delicate gauze.

The wind keened around the corners of the barn, rattling the door, threatening the flame in the lantern, and the mare lurched to her feet, nuzzled the newborn, and began licking it, learning its taste and scent, warming the frail body with her own.

Clytie sighed. "It's always magic. Seeing this, I always believe."

"In what?"

She shrugged. "In good things. This is one. There have to be others."

In the pale light she seemed too fragile to take on the life that she was leading, that waited to crush her and her beliefs. He didn't want to see her broken, old before her time like so many others, but he guessed that, if he reached out now and took her in his arms, the lioness in her would fight. She was proud, with the memory of the dead husband still fresh, and he was only a stranger come in out of the storm, the link between them too newly forged. With an effort, he turned back to the mare and the colt that was struggling to stand on its too slender legs, on hoofs that were hard rubber.

"You ought to name him Storm," he said, and was amazed that he sounded like himself, with none of the ragged edges of desire in his voice.

A smile shattered her face. "I will. He'll grow into it. He's already a fighter."

"Like you."

"I do what I have to." She reached for the lantern. "Best leave them to it. You come back to the house. You must be hungry."

He was, and not just for food. Not even just for a woman. A whole segment of his life was missing, used up, gone. He was Lyle Speaks, but he wasn't sure who that was or who he'd been. There wasn't much good to remember, now that he reflected on it. Not much good at all. To cover his emotion he said: "Just don't point that shotgun at me while I eat."

She smiled again, and he saw fine lines beside her eyes where the smile lingered. "I won't. And I'm sorry I acted like I did. I just have to be careful."

"You did right. You're alone, but you shouldn't be."

She ignored that, struggling to open the door against the wind. He put his shoulder to it, pushed, and felt the force take him, wipe out the feeble lantern flame so they were alone in the whirling dark.

She took his hand. "Come on!"

The drifts were over his knees. By morning

they'd be lucky to be able to walk. He'd have to stay. Make sure she had enough wood for the fire, a path shoveled between the barn and the house — a man's work, even if she did wield a shotgun with the best of them.

The cabin was one large room, the sleeping part separated from the rest by a blanket hung over a line. He saw clothes hanging neatly from pegs, the shotgun replaced beside the door, and a big stone fireplace where flames still flickered, casting warmth and light and shadow.

She poured water into a basin. "You can wash up."

The water was warm, having stood on the hearth, a luxury, he thought, as this little room was a luxury, with its pine table, rag rug, and Clytie moving briskly from kettle to cupboard. All that was lacking was a stiff shot of whisky, peddlers or no.

As if she'd read his mind, she put a jug and a glass on the table. "It's legal. I keep it handy as medicine, although Drew liked a drink now and again."

"Your husband?"

She nodded, her back turned.

"How long were you married?"

"Not long enough." She jerked her shoulders straight.

He saw her quick movement and understood. You fought for what you wanted, believed in, and then it was taken without your knowledge or acceptance. And then you fought again, regardless of circumstances or sex.

He said: "You could go back, you know. Some place easier than this."

She turned on him, yellow eyes fiery. "To what? To being an orphan? To being somebody's slave? You can talk all you want, Mister Speaks, but there's no way in hell I'll go back." The light in her eyes softened. "Out here I'm free. Working for myself. You ought to be able to understand that, being a man. And, besides, I'm not built for towns, and I don't much like company, especially the female kind." She gave a short laugh. "And I find that females don't much care for me, either."

Maybe it was the whisky, maybe it was how she looked — defiant — or maybe the thought of her ready to blast him with a shotgun. Whatever, Lyle threw back his head and laughed.

"Don't you laugh at me!" She slammed a bowl down in front of him.

He stopped as quickly as he'd started. She had a temper, and Christ knew what she'd do if provoked. "I'm not laughing at you, Clytie Beck. I was laughing at all the city females I've known. There's not a one could hold a candle to you." Painted women, whores, church-goers, schoolteachers, and every one had wanted to tame him, change him, put him in a suit of clothes to fit their image, just like they'd try to do to Clytie, and with as much chance of success.

"I don't fit," she said. "Except out here."

She'd fit in his arms. The whole golden length

of her, supple as a cat and just as untamed. For the first time in his life, Lyle held back. A woman like this one couldn't be taken. She had to come on her own, had to be courted, but not in the way it was usually done, with flowers and poetry and cautious hand holding. For a minute he wondered if he were crazy, if he were equal to the task, and then he chuckled.

"You fit fine," he said. "How long till supper?"

She woke with a start in the middle of the night and lay still, listening. The wind howled, but the house was silent except for Lyle's steady breathing beyond the curtain that was all that separated them. Judging from the sound, he was asleep. She relaxed then, amazed at herself for actually permitting him to stay in the house — a stranger and a dangerous man if she was any judge. *But not to me,* she thought. *He'll never hurt me,* and then wondered why she was so certain of it.

Nothing he'd said exactly. More the way he'd acted, how he listened when she talked, understood her need for caution, even what appeared to be her bad manners but was only self-defense. And several times she'd caught him watching her with something like sadness in his eyes — and something else that made her catch her breath and turn away to hide the leap of her own heart.

She was, she admitted, lonely for talk with someone other than herself, her horses, and Lyle's presence had eased the emptiness, the threat of storm. They had talked about everything, although she suspected he'd left out a large chunk of his life, glossed over it as if he were ashamed or wanted to spare her. That was all right. Half the people out here had lives they never mentioned, secrets that they kept, names they hadn't been born with. Even she didn't know her own, true name. They'd found her at the door of the church and taken her in, called her by the name scrawled on a torn piece of brown paper. **Clytie,** the message said. **One month and six days.** No more.

Well, someone had cared enough to give her one name and a birthday, to leave her where she'd be found and cared for. Somewhere she had a mother and a father, a family she'd imagined over and over throughout childhood; a house with high ceilings and polished wooden floors, a house filled with love and the scent of cookies baking, as unlike the orphanage as heaven was unlike hell.

She'd been tall for her age, and strong. At fourteen she'd been taken by a farmer and his wife who needed cheap labor, and labor it was. They worked her hard. Sometimes she was almost too tired to eat the food that was, at least, plentiful. Sometimes she dreamed of running away, but she had no place to run to, no safe haven except those she created in her mind.

From the woman she'd learned thrift and how to run a house. From the man the ways of a farm and its animals, and she found she had a knack with animals, something more than simple liking, as if she and they shared a language not understood by others. That was how she'd met Drew and changed her life forever.

The wagon train had stopped near the creek at the bottom pasture to make repairs and give the stock a chance to graze. Andrew Beck had been with the train, a man with a purpose. He was going to Montana to raise horses, and he was bringing his own stud, a black Thoroughbred from Kentucky that he'd named Roamer. An apt name as it turned out, for he'd broken loose and come to the barn where she'd been milking, came with flashing eyes and raised tail, following a scent on the evening air. She'd never seen anything more beautiful, more powerful, more sure of itself than the stallion, but, unafraid, she'd gone out and picked up the frayed rope that dangled from the halter.

"Where'd you come from?" she'd asked, and grinned when he arched his neck and blew.

"Think a lot of yourself, don't you? Think you can just come up here and raise Cain. Well you can't. I bet somebody is missing you and fit to be tied, so come on. I'll take you back." And she hadn't been surprised when he had followed her, hadn't had the sense to realize she was leading potential death on a string.

It was like it had been meant from the beginning, Drew coming out to meet her, to take the stallion and tether him, and then to ask her questions, all the while looking at her as if he couldn't get enough.

She hadn't known about passion. What she wanted, had always wanted, was to belong somewhere, to someone. So when Drew asked her, she'd made up her mind in an instant, had gone with him, and never looked back. Until now, with the stranger asleep by the hearth, the man she'd taken in because he was as lonely as she and didn't know it. Because they were both drifting, even though she was rooted here in this place she'd helped to build, drifting like smoke, belonging to no one, and aching inside.

How would it be to be with a man again? *This* man, lean of body, with cheek bones she wanted to touch? How would it feel not to sleep alone any more, to give up her secrets at the moment of joining?

Lyle Speaks. Her lips formed the words. *Lyle Speaks.* A name, a sound to hold to in the dark.

The wind died as she lay thinking, replaced by a silence as deep as the bottom of a well. She listened, heard Lyle's steady breathing, and snow sifting against the small window. Far off, a wolf howled, hungry and hunting in spite of storm, lured by instinct to those struggling in the drifts, weak, trapped, dying.

She hoped Drew had been dead before they'd got to him. Hoped he'd not spent his last minutes fighting them off, calling her name, and her too far away to hear.

The howling was closer now, and her thoughts turned to the foal. Had she shut the barn door, or had they left it open in their struggle with the wind? Wolves had come in before, after her chickens, come right up to the house on padded paws, and she had met them with the shotgun, just like she was going to do now. She slipped out of bed, searched for her moccasins, grabbed the buffalo coat that doubled as blanket, and moved toward the door.

No need to wake the stranger. She'd handle this herself like always. The door opened easily on leather hinges, and she saw that the snow had stopped, leaving only a few horse-tail clouds and a moon reflecting off the ground. Her shadow moved before her, black on silver and long, as if she were a giantess moving soundlessly toward other shadows that materialized out of nowhere.

The path she'd made earlier was obliterated. In one step she was up to her waist, floundering, trying to keep from falling, to keep hold of the shotgun that was her only defense against the wolves moving stealthily across the yard.

Now where was she going at this time of night, tip-toeing past him like a slender ghost? Lyle watched her pick up the shotgun and open the door, saw the moonlight beyond and the path it made into the house, saw her silhouetted against it, a proper target if she'd stopped to think.

In one quick motion he was out of his bedroll and on his feet, pistol in hand. She hadn't asked for any help, but that was how she was made —

independent as a hog on ice. When he reached the door, he saw her fighting the snow, saw the wolves, six of them, drawn by her struggle, sure of an easy kill, and he shot — once, twice, three times — heard the yelps as they leaped and went down. Then he was pushing toward her as best he could through the drifts.

"What in hell do you think you're doing?" Fear turned his voice harsh.

Her teeth were chattering when she answered, as much from shock as from cold. "I couldn't remember if we shut the barn. Help me out before I freeze."

"What if I hadn't been here?"

"Well, you were."

"And that's no answer." Damn, she didn't weigh much more than a bird, he thought as he hauled her up and carried her to the house.

"It was the best I could do," she said, shivering in spite of herself.

"I'll check the barn. You go warm up. Take off those wet moccasins." And if she got sick, what would happen? She'd be here alone, tending the animals, killing herself to do what she had to.

He stopped to inspect the wolves. They were big ones, with fine pelts. In the morning, after the fleas had jumped off in search of a better home, he'd skin them. They'd make a warm coat, or a rug for beside her bed. Her bed. He'd wanted to be in it, but had forced himself to move slowly. If he hadn't, none of this nonsense would have happened. With that, he made up his

88

mind. When he left here, she was going with him, although how he was going to convince her he couldn't figure.

The door to the barn was closed, but he opened it and peered in, waiting for his eyes to adjust to the darkness. The mares were both on their feet, alerted to danger, but the foal, curled up in straw, slept the deep, dreamless sleep of the very young.

"Reckon they won't be back tonight, Mama," he said. "You and your baby are safe." And she nickered at him with a gentle flaring of her nostrils.

He slogged back to the cabin. Clytie had been right to go out and defend. The loss of brood mares like these, even without the foal, would, indeed, have been a disaster. But damn it! Why hadn't she called for help?

She was standing by the fire in her stocking feet. The hem of her skirt was wet, and her hair had come loose from its tight braid, giving her the look of a girl, young and vulnerable.

"That was a damn' fool stunt." He closed the door behind him and drew the bar. "You should've called me."

"You needed your sleep."

"I've gone without before. Did you stop to think what would have happened if I hadn't been around?"

"Yes." Her voice was small.

He folded his arms across his chest and looked at her. "I have a suggestion."

"What?" She returned his look with a hint of suspicion, as if she knew what he was going to say and was ready to counter it.

"Come with me when I leave."

She opened her mouth, then closed it, and turned away and stared into the fire for a long moment.

It struck him that she might be hiding tears, and he went to stand beside her. "I didn't mean. . . ."

When she turned back, her eyes were bright, but with anger. "I know what you meant. You're not the first or the last to ask me, Mister Speaks. But I'll be no man's whore. I've done fine on my own, and I don't need you to feel sorry, to feel you can just walk in here with your hands out and think I'll fall into your arms." Then she was quiet, chewing on her bottom lip, hating herself for being at cross-purposes.

He sighed. He might have known she'd take it that way, should have realized she'd reject what he hadn't said right in the first place.

"Clytie. . . ."

"What?"

"I'm sorry."

She sniffed. "You'd better be. Coming in here, acting like all you have to do is snap your fingers and I'll follow you. Like I haven't any brains or self-respect."

"You've got plenty of both."

"So you say now." She poked at the fire and watched it, ignoring him.

He'd lived most of his life in the company of men — and liked it that way. He'd not wanted to be tied down, leg-shackled to some female who expected him to be different than what he was. Nor had he ever wanted to give his heart to anyone. Not after losing it once. Yet, in a few brief hours, all that had changed, and on account of this woman who'd opened up his past and shared her own, and in so doing had laid it all to rest.

And, damn, she was beautiful, with the spill of yellow hair catching the firelight, and her determined little chin set hard, trying not to show her hurt.

He'd come to Montana for a second chance, a new life, and here she was, the woman he wanted to share it with, only he'd made a mess of the whole thing.

"We'd make a pair, Clytie," he said slowly, reaching deep into his head for the right words. They were long in coming. He put his hands on her shoulders, expecting her to pull away, but she didn't, just stood where she was, still as a hunted animal, waiting.

"I came here to start over," he said finally. "To find a little peace and to settle. To build something I'd be proud of and maybe pass on. But I can't do it alone. A man needs a woman. A wife. Just like a woman needs a man. It's good not to fight alone, to have somebody watching your back who cares, who's there in bad times and good ones. You and me, we're both loners, but maybe we've had enough. Maybe it's time to try another way. That's what I meant in the first place, only I haven't had much practice asking."

Her tears came then, big ones, along with a chuckle. "That's about the prettiest proposal I've ever heard." Not only that, it was only the second one, but best not to admit that much. She wiped her face with her sleeve. "I need time to think. We only just met." Oh, she knew her answer. It just wasn't seemly to accept too fast, like you hadn't an alternative, were so man-hungry you'd take any one that came along.

His hands tightened on her arms, then went around her. "How much time?"

"A month?" Her words were muffled against his shoulder.

"Too long."

She fit against him like a hand in a glove. He tilted her face to his. "I'm not a patient man, Clytie. I've waited most of my life, but no more."

When he kissed her, she thought that she'd been waiting, too — for the surge of fire deep in her belly that was so strong she was startled and drew back.

He felt her response and tightened his hold. "Well?"

A few hours before she'd been drifting like smoke, and now she was flame, and suddenly she recognized that without it there was nothing between a man and a woman, only words and meaningless couplings, and that she could grow old, embittered, out of simple pride.

Even knowing her answer, she held firm. "A month. That way you'll have time to change your mind."

"I won't."

She shrugged. "It's a possibility."

"You're stubborn."

"See! You're finding fault already." She turned away so he couldn't see her regret. "Drew never minded."

Was she comparing them? he wondered. *Making a saint out of a dead man, and himself falling short?*

"Neither do I," he said. "Sometimes stubbornness is a good thing."

"If I wasn't, I wouldn't be here," she said, acknowledging her efforts to keep what she had, to keep going, regardless. "So you can add pride to the list."

"Anything else I should know?" He was laughing now, and she heard it, risked a look over her shoulder.

"You'll have to find out for yourself," she said, flirting a little before turning prickly again. "Now I'm going back to sleep, and so should you."

"Alone?"

"Mister Speaks. . . ."

"Lyle."

"What happened before wasn't an invitation." Although she wished it were, wished the night and the storm would go on forever, and the two of them here, the world with its rules and regulations non-existent.

She was tough, honest, straight-talking. What was generally called "a good woman." Funny how, after all these years, he'd fallen for a replica of what he'd respected in his childhood; how all the women he'd known since were no more than faces without names.

He said: "You drive a hard bargain."

Her eyes caught the gleam of the fire. "Things that come easy usually aren't worth it."

"You have an answer for everything."

Did she? Was she shutting him out with an answer, or only a temporary retreat? "Not everything. Not for this. I don't even understand what happened, or if I can trust myself."

"Do you trust me?"

She looked at him a long time before answering with a quick nod of her head. "Yes." That was all. She pulled the blanket that divided the room, closing herself in, shutting him out.

He sat looking into the coals, fighting the heat of his desire. It would be easy to go to her, wrestle her down, take her. But what then? He'd never make it up to her. She'd never forgive or forget, and he'd have lost what he knew he wanted above any momentary passion.

"Damn you, Clytie," he murmured, and had the suspicion it wasn't the last time he'd say it. One thing sure, with her around, he'd never be bored. He wondered what Sam was going to say when he found him hitched, and to a lady who not only knew her own mind but said it, straight out. And then he wondered what he'd do if, at the end of a month, she turned him down.

From the top of the rise he looked back. She stood in the yard, hands clasped, a small figure, too small to be left alone. By chance or luck, he'd found her, the woman he'd been waiting for without knowing it, and to lose her now would be like killing that part of himself that had just come to life.

"It's only a month," she'd said that morning, when he tried once more to change her mind. "You have things to do, and so do I, so stop fussing."

But anything could happen in a month. Hell, life could change from one minute to the next. Courage and determination were well and good, but she was female, a target for any Indian, any horse thief that came along, even if she was good with that shotgun. And of all the women in the world, he had to pick one who didn't know the meaning of fear.

He lifted a hand. Waved. She waved back, her arm high in the air in a gesture that seemed triumphant.

He nudged the roan and went on, following a faint trail beside the river. The worst of the snow had melted, turning the ground to mud, the prairie grasses green, and in spite of his worries Lyle responded as any cattleman would. Here was all the grass anyone needed — miles of it, unfenced, unsurveyed, free for the taking.

Here was his future, spread out around him and full of promise.

A bunch of antelope, startled at his approach, bounded away, white rumps flashing, and in the muck at the river edge, frogs twanged, croaked, shrilled, a pulsing chorus, urgent and insistent. It seemed the whole earth was in a frenzy of regeneration.

He put the roan to a swinging trot, eager to get to what he now thought of as home. Yet, when he saw the cabin in the distance, his heart sank. Compared to Clytie's snug place, this was a disaster, a windowless shack, lacking a door and leaning at an angle as if a good wind could push it over. Hardly a place to bring a bride, a woman whose own house boasted a fireplace, a wooden floor, a window of real glass.

Working alone, felling enough timber, always conscious of the threat of Indians and taking precautions, he'd be lucky to get a few logs laid in a month. And if at that time she refused him, what then? No matter how you looked at it, women created problems. Come to it, life was full of problems, regardless of where you were or what you did. He had expected starting a cattle operation would be easy, but all by himself he'd introduced complications.

· He looked around the little valley, rimmed by hills, cut by the river, with a creek to the east. The frogs still twanged like a thousand jew's harps, and a lark rose up out of the grass singing. It was a fine place, peaceful in itself, well-regulated. It was humans and their greed who brought trouble into paradise, and he expected that sooner or later he'd see trouble enough.

For now, he'd sat dreaming too long. "Reckon I'd best get started," he said, and swung down off the roan.

The shot went over his head, missing him by inches. A second earlier, and he'd have been dead. The horse shied, but he held onto the rein, keeping the animal between himself and whoever was out there — someone who had every intention of killing him.

Cautiously he maneuvered around the side of the cabin, thinking fast. Once behind the shack, he'd be able to get to his rifle in its scabbard on the other side of the roan. Then, with luck, he'd cut through the brush and locate his attackers. They had obviously been here a while, judging from the churned-up ground and horse droppings. Three of them, he decided, and white, riding shod animals. Maybe Clytie's whisky peddlers working a still.

"But not for long," he said, tying the horse and slipping the Winchester out of the scabbard. Then soft-footed as an Indian, he ducked into the brush and crouched down, listening. Frogs. The sound of the creek running over rocks, his own breathing, slow and steady. *Come on, you bastards.*

Somewhere up ahead a horse blew. Still he waited. Sooner or later they'd move, show themselves, and he was patient, the hunter waiting, silent behind a screen of elders, primed for the kill.

Clytie watched him disappear over the rise, then stood a long time examining the turn her life had taken without any warning at all. Only two days before she'd been someone else, a woman without hope or feelings, going through the motions of life by rote, seeking only the rude means of survival, talking to herself to break the silence, falling asleep out of exhaustion and ignoring the emptiness of bed and heart.

And then Lyle had come out of the storm, a man like any other, or so she'd believed until that moment when he looked at the mare, and she'd seen compassion in his eyes, a rare understanding of nature and the pain of living. He was tough, with a hard shell around his pain that was similar to hers. She'd sensed that, known it through instinct, the way an animal recognizes its likeness and responds. There was a bleakness in him, well-hidden except to her who had tasted bitter despair, the finality of death, the horror of it. Even now she remembered how Drew had looked. Mouth open in what was a last cry of agony, the bones of face and body, plainly visible, brown bleaching to ivory, returning to dust.

Standing there in the yard, she shuddered, clenched her hands into fists. Just like this, she'd waved Drew off and then had gone about her chores with a will. Just like this she'd been certain he'd come back, sure of the rhythm and continuity of her days. Did actions repeat? Had she, hung up on her pride, her doubts, sent Lyle off to a similar end?

"You stop right now," she said, and even to herself she sounded puny, a lone voice staving off terror. This was what happened when you let down your guard, allowed yourself to feel. Oh, she should never have let him in her house — or her heart. She'd made a mistake and now would suffer for it.

"Damn you, Lyle Speaks," she said, and was pleased that she sounded herself again, the Clytie with her head on straight.

She turned on her heel and went to the barn, let the mare and foal out and watched as the youngster tried his legs, investigated the piles of drifted snow, and jumped at the sight of his own shadow.

Storm, Lyle had named him, right after his birth. Lyle again. In three days he'd stamped everything with his mark. Even her. Especially her. And now a month seemed infinity — thirty years instead of thirty days, and each one more worrisome than the last.

In the house, too, were reminders — the whisky jug, the remains of breakfast, wood he had carried in and stacked by the hearth — and something else, the scents of leather, tobacco, maleness.

Would he come back? Or would she be left waiting, faithful, all the long years of her life, looking out over the plains for the sight of one who never came?

She cleared the plates, swept the crumbs from the table, then attacked the floor with a broom, and her thoughts danced like dust motes in the light from the open door. A part of her was riding with him on the trail north, where the future lay in wait, a panther crouched, ready to spring. Her hands clenched on the broom handle. She had never been superstitious, never believed in the spiritualism that had taken such a hold on so many, but she had learned to trust her instinct, that mysterious sensing of people and possibilities that was warning her now.

Quickly she undressed, pulled on Drew's trousers and shirt, a wool jacket, heavy boots. The old pistol was stuck in her belt, and the shells put into deep pockets. She saddled the brown mare, threw hay for the new mother and grain for the chickens in the coop next to the house, then she picked up the shotgun and closed the door.

"I'm coming." The wind took her voice, carried it off like a tumbleweed, split it into syllables, untranslatable sound.

Lyle's trail was plain. She found where he'd stopped and rested the horses, and where a party of Indians had crossed behind him, hesitating, then going on their way. The brown mare had an easy, ground-covering jog and was tireless, but it was mid-afternoon before she pulled up on the hill that looked down into the valley and heard the shots—the crack of a rifle answered by a flurry of bullets from her side of the creek and a second rifle shot.

Lyle, she thought. And not in the cabin but hidden somewhere. She scanned the course of the creek, steep-sided and overgrown, and on the wind, faint but unmistakable, she caught the scent of fermenting grain.

"God-damned whisky traders! God-damned murdering bastards!" And Lyle was out there alone, probably across the creek, judging from the sound of the rifle.

A flash of blue caught her eyes, and she squinted, straining to see through the undergrowth. They'd chosen their hiding place well. No one passing by would notice the little camp, not unless the smell was obvious.

"The odds just got a little better," she said, and smiled grimly. Then she led the mare downstream, tied her, and walked cautiously back up the rise.

Her choices were plain. She could swing around and find Lyle, or she could come up behind the bastards, catching them unaware. Without hesitation she chose the latter, slipping into the underbrush like a shadow, finding and following a narrow but well-used trail. Obviously they'd been here over the winter, spreading their trash around, replenishing their supply of rotgut, thumbing their noses at the law. And on Lyle's place! She clenched her jaw. "I'll see you in hell. Every last one." The words were soundless but felt, a cold anger that steeled every muscle, pulsed in her veins, urged her on so she had to force herself to go quietly.

Intent on watching where she put her feet, she almost walked into the small clearing where the three men were crouched, their attention on the opposite bank. Behind them she caught sight of a rude still, and farther back three horses, probably stolen. They were fine animals, too fine for the likes of these. Cautiously she backed away, ducked behind a boulder, and considered her options once more. She could go back in shooting and hope to get them before they turned on her, but that seemed foolish. Dying wasn't part of her plan, or being held hostage, either.

A crackle of brush, heavy footsteps turned her mouth dry. Had they found her out already? She flattened herself against the stone, drawing the pistol. One of the men, tall, with a filthy red beard, came around the bend carrying a rifle. Because of trash like him, Drew was dead, and who knew how many others. She lay still, holding her breath, as he passed without a glance. All of his attention was on the opposite bank where Lyle was holed up. Probably his rifle fire had given him away, and now this man was intending to circle around, cross the creek. Well, not if she had anything to do about it! Silently she followed, realizing that, if her prey went too far downstream, he'd find the mare and come back looking for the rider.

"You just do that," she muttered. "You just come on back. I'll be here waiting."

Lyle waded across the creek that was running

high in the spring run-off, to the east bank. Cover was thinner on that side, but he found a cottonwood with a double trunk and crept behind it. He'd been in worse situations, but few as uncomfortable as this one. The ground was damp, the wind was rising, his boots were soaked. The night would be long and cold — and sleepless if he couldn't pick off his attackers in daylight. There had to be a way to bring them out into the open.

A movement that wasn't part of the brush caught his eye. Either they'd gotten careless, or they figured he'd gone. A mistake, he thought, as he sighted down the barrel of the Winchester, taking his time, aiming at the target that was now still. A volley of shots answered his fire, all going wild. He squeezed off another, then looked around, assessing his options. Now, at least, he had them located, could make a move instead of sitting here, wasting shells. He looked downstream, searching for a better place to cross, and saw Clytie walking slowly up the hill, coming into trouble sure as she was born. And there was no way he could warn her, call out, without putting her in greater danger.

She had to have heard the shots, must know she was walking into a rattlesnake den. For a long moment she stood looking around, searching both sides of the creek, and it seemed that her eyes met his, that he could see their yellow light, fearless, as if she knew his predicament and had come to help. Cat-footed, carrying the shotgun, she disappeared, moving in the direction of the still, and he took comfort from the stealth of her movements. She wasn't a fool, and she was well-armed. But she was on her own. All he could do was trust her judgment. And if anything went wrong, he'd take her killers apart with his bare hands. With that, he waited, his thoughts bitter, his intentions fueled by controlled rage. How many times was it possible to lose what you loved before even the future had no more promise and you gave up, quit living?

Suddenly a man stepped out part way out of the brush, and, behind him, off to one side, was Clytie, pistol in hand. Lyle fired a second before she did, and watched his quarry fall, face down in the muck of the creek.

"Clytie!"

She threw up her head, then motioned for silence, and faded back, Indian-like, into the weeds.

Admiration for her replaced his anger. With a woman like this a man could take on anything — Indians, outlaws, a platoon of peddlers. And she was his. Or was she? Dammit! Her very presence was a distraction, with at least two of the bastards still holed up like bears in a den. But if he were any judge, they'd soon come to find out what had happened to their partner, show themselves, and get shot down for their trouble. So again he waited, this time knowing he had an ally on the other side — a yellow-eyed woman dressed as a man, with a braid down her back as thick as her arm.

Only one of the men came, creeping down the trail, searching the woods on either side, forgetting caution when he spied the dead man half in the water.

"Bert!" he called over his shoulder to his unseen partner, then rushed out and bent over the body.

Like picking cans off a wall, Lyle thought, and smiled as he watched the second man jerk and fall beside his comrade.

Two down. One to go. He prayed Clytie didn't miss. A minute passed. Then two. He strained to see, then began creeping down the steep bank, heedless of the fact that he was now a perfect target. The shotgun roared.

Reaching the creek, he waded across, paying no attention to the water that came to his knees, stopping to check the two bodies. Both dead, but he took no chances, pitching their rifles into the brush, taking the pistols they had stuck in their belts. Quite a collection — one worth keeping in a place like this one was turning out to be.

At a sound behind him, he whirled, his own pistol cocked.

"It's me!" Her hat was gone. She had a scratch on one cheek, and her hair had come loose, but her eyes glowed, pieces of topaz, the creek with the sun on it.

"Don't you ever come sneaking up on me like that again." Fright turned his voice hoarse. He'd nearly killed her himself.

"That's a fine thank you." She shifted the shotgun and stood there, legs planted, oddly appealing in her man's clothing.

"Why'd you come?" He had to know.

She frowned, then shook her shoulders as if ridding herself of an unwanted, invisible weight. "It was like I knew there was trouble. When it got so I couldn't wait it out, I came. Guess I was right." Her grin was cocky but suddenly lopsided. "The other one's back there. I killed him. I never killed anybody before." Now that she had time to think, all she could see was the last man, his head blown apart. Her doing. She swallowed hard.

"It's done." Lyle put his arms around her.

She went on as if she hadn't heard. "I didn't think how it would be. All I thought about was living instead of dying. Of them, those bastards, and how nobody was going to take anything else away from me. They had no right, them and their stinking still, lining their pockets on other folks' grief. Except I never figured his brains would fly all over. I never thought about that part at all."

She buried her face in his shoulder, and he could feel her heart pounding like a drum. He remembered how he'd felt after stabbing the Comanche — as if he'd puke out his guts, as if he was somebody else who belonged nowhere, had no name or purpose.

Vindication brought its own curse that was often harder to bear than revenge. She'd be seeing the dead man in her dreams for a long time, and he'd be seeing the determination on her face as she stalked into the woods, shotgun in hand, a woman defending her own.

"Why'd you come?" he asked again, softly, into her ear.

She pushed away and looked up at him, struggling to find the words to explain, not only to him but to herself. It was hard saying what was simply there, what she had no name for. Finally she said: "If you'd never come back, I couldn't have stood it. There's only so much waiting a woman can do. You said how a man and a woman should go on together, in bad times and good, and I figured this was one of those bad times. I reckon I was right."

"Reckon you were at that," he said. "Does this mean the month is over?"

Again he watched as she seemed to retreat into some inner world only she could reach, and he guessed it would always be this way, her with secret places denied him. But wasn't that true of everyone, himself included?

Still, as he'd told her, he wasn't a patient man. He tightened his hold on her and saw the beginning of a smile, the crinkling of the fine lines at the corners of her eyes.

"Well?"

The smile shivered across her face. "Life's too short as it is," she said. "A month is a plain waste of time."

"Amen to that."

And, after all, how simple it was when you'd

taken the right way, made the correct choice.

"All I've got to offer is a shack," he said. "For right now."

"I've been worse places." She looked around, then took his hand. "Let's go home," she said.

Wild Flower

I am indebted to Eleanor Mueller and Bruce Robinson, grandniece and nephew of Louisa Houston, for preserving her letters; to Earp historian Glenn Boyer who recognized their importance and first published them in 1981 in an article entitled, "Morgan Earp, Brother in the Shadow," and to Lyman B. Hanley and Lyman L. Hanley, nephew and grandnephew of Louisa for their interest, advice, tireless research, and friendship. Of particular interest to me reading through these letters was what seemed to be left out, supplanted by Louisa's preoccupation with flowers and scenery to the exclusion of almost all else. Eventually, however, I realized that Louisa Houston and her sisters were typical Victorians, and that Victorian women, even one married to an Earp, were excluded from the world of men and communicated in a kind of code, which in Louisa's case dealt with collecting and pressing flowers, making quilts, and sending locks of hair home, probably to be made into jewelry as was common custom. In writing "Wild Flower," I have attempted to be true to Louisa's style of writing and outlook, filling in gaps in her life with fictional letters. When I have used her actual letters, they appear in quotes.

Deadwood, South Dakota, 1876
Dear Sister Kate:

It is hard to describe how cold it is here. In memory Iowa seems warm compared to Deadwood. We have had blizzards, and the town is completely snowed in, so I don't know when this letter will reach you. Maybe by spring!

I was glad to hear that you are happy with your husband and family. When you and I ran away, we had no idea what would happen to us, but it seemed like it would be a great adventure. For me it has been. Life with Morgan is never dull, and with his brothers Wyatt and Virgil and their wives here with us, there's always a lot of laughter and companionship. We are a real family. There are friends of Morgan's in town, too, a Doctor and Mrs. Holliday. He's a dentist, and she's a foreigner but a nice lady. The two of them fight a lot, I'm not sure why, except it seems like they each want something from the other that they can't have. I know that doesn't make sense, but that's the way it looks to me.

The doctor and Morgan and Wyatt are all good friends and go out a lot in the evenings, and Kate, that's the doctor's wife, comes over, and we drink coffee and talk, and she tells stories about the old country and Mexico that sound so real it's as good as seeing pictures of those places.

Wyatt has some idea about going to Dodge City when the snow melts, but Morgan isn't interested. He says he wants to see the country, that there are lots of places he wants to take me that I will like because he knows how much I love scenery and flowers.

We came here through beautiful country. The leaves were turning, and the prairie grass was gold, and once a fox ran nearly under the horses' feet, a splendid sight with his tail so bushy it seemed to drag on the ground.

In spite of the cold and snow, Deadwood is lively, always something going on. There are theatrical performances at the Bella Union and the Gem theaters, and the gambling places never close, and there are lots of Chinese living here who are very colorful and interesting to watch. Some of the women have tiny feet, no bigger than a baby's, and they can't walk very well, but then it isn't easy to walk here on the best of days, what with ice and snow and the freight wagons taking up the whole street in good weather. One of the drivers is a woman, a Madam Canutson, who dresses like a man and cusses like one, too. I can't write any of what she said in a letter. She turned the air blue.

Then there's the woman everybody calls Calamity Jane. They say she was in love with Wild Bill Hickok who was shot and killed just before we came. Now she drags herself around, usually drunk, and very sad. I feel sorry for her because she's got nobody and we all need somebody to care for.

Well, I've gone on rambling for long enough.

Give my love to everybody, and I'll write again soon.

Your loving sister,
Louisa Houston Earp

Butte, Montana, 1879
Dear Sister Kate:

Time goes so fast, especially when you're sick. I can't remember when I wrote last and don't know where I've put your letter.

Since I took sick that first winter, I haven't been right. They said I had rheumatic fever, whatever that is. I thought I would die, and sometimes I wish I had. There are days I can't get out of bed and lie there thinking about how different life might have been.

I might never have left home, got married, raised a family, never gone farther away than Mason City. But then I wouldn't have met Morgan, who is so good to me. And I wouldn't have gotten to see so many wonderful things — things that have sustained me in my illness.

When we first came here, Morgan was driving freight and ore wagons, but when I was so ill, he quit to stay closer to home. But the money run out, and now he's on the police force, and we have a miner's wife, Mrs. Pospisil, who comes in and cooks and looks out for me. She's nice enough, but so healthy I wish she'd go away. I hate being sick, and it's not fair to Morgan. All the Earps are healthy as horses, never sick for a minute, or if they are, they don't pay any attention.

I can't tell you what life in a mining town is like. There are always fights and thieves after the gold. It's not like farming. There's never any of the peace and good times we knew, and I'm fearful all the time that something will happen to Morgan and I'll be left here.

Before I took sick, we had such good times. We'd go out into the country and pick flowers, big bunches, and bring them home. I put them in jars and buckets to brighten up the house, but they never lasted long enough. Maybe we should have left them where they were. Maybe that's the trouble. They didn't belong here.

I saved some seeds which I'm sending along. You might try to grow them and think of me. I think of everybody back home a lot and cherish the little pressed honeysuckle you sent to me.

Please pass my love along and take some for yourself. If I ever get well, I'll be home for a visit. If I don't, these letters will have to do. And the flower seeds. So many colors! I never thought there were so many colors in this world.

Your loving sister,
Louisa Houston Earp

Temescal, California, March 5, 1880
Dear Sister Agnes:

"I take my pen in hand to let you know where I am. We arrived in San Bernardino on Wednesday evening and Thursday came by train to the Temescal Mountains Warm Springs."

Morgan's parents run the hotel and baths here, and I like them very much. Once again I have a family. Morgan's mother is a fine cook, and she promised to teach me some of her recipes when I am feeling better. His father is a wonderful gentleman who escorts all of the women visitors with a great flourish.

My health was one reason we left Montana. I never quite got better, and when I looked in the mirror I got a shock. I don't think you would recognize me, though Morgan says I'm prettier than I was when we met in Kansas. He can say nice things sometimes, just like his father.

Like when we were on our way here and passed near Salt Lake City, and I was teasing him and said maybe he'd ought to become a Mormon and get another wife that wasn't sickly. He just laughed and said I suited him fine, sick or well. Made me feel good just hearing him.

Some of the country we came through was so beautiful it took my breath. I spent nights just looking out the window at the desert with the moon shining on it. The moon is so bright, you'd almost think it was day, only everything it touches turns silver, for miles and miles, like a kind of fairy tale. The view made me forget how uncomfortable the train was, with the smoke coming in, and the dust and ashes, and there were passengers with crying babies and some men who hadn't had a bath since before the snow fell sitting across from us, and if the moon hadn't taken my breath, they would have!

No sense dwelling on that. The good thing is that we're here at Temescal, and I think the warm weather and the mineral baths should restore my health very soon.

Please give my love to everybody.

Your sister,
Louisa Houston Earp

Temescal, California, April, 1880

Dear Agnes:

If you could only see how everything here grows and blooms. I wish I could paint pictures or write so that you could understand. My head is full of what I see, but my body does not have the strength or the knowledge of how to tell you. All I can do is look and fill my eyes, and collect flowers and seeds and the shells I am enclosing with this letter.

A week ago I finally got to the coast and saw the ocean, which I was wanting to do. But when at last I stood there on the sand looking out to where it met the sky, it was too big to understand, bigger than anything I've ever seen. It was bright blue, and green, and all colors in between, and just before the waves broke, the inside of them was gray with light shining through. They made me feel as small as a grain of the sand under my feet. After a while I turned my back on the water and searched for shells. So many! So small! I filled my pockets with them, and Morgan filled his, and they jingled all the way home like little bells. Life goes on regardless of oceans or wickedness or people's cruelty.

I am not talking about my life here, but about what goes on in a world we don't know about but that I know is out there waiting.

With love,
Your sister Louisa

Temescal, California, May, 1880
Dear Sister Agnes:

I take my pen in hand to write you on this very pretty morning. The hills around are covered with flowers. I don't know the names of all of them, but have planted some around the place and they have come up, and I pressed some in a magazine which I am sending to you.

It is very nice here, though Morgan doesn't have work and is restless living off his folks. He is thinking of going to Arizona where his brothers are and leaving me here a while.

I have grown quite fond of his parents, especially his father who keeps all the guests happy and laughing. He is a fine singer, and sometimes in the evenings entertains with hymns and the songs we sang when we were growing up. He is particularly vain about his appearance and his beard, washes it every morning in lemon verbena soap, so when he gives me a hug, and he always does, it's very pleasant, not like some of the men we knew whose beards always smelled awful.

Morgan's mother, I think I told you, is a fine cook, one of the reasons I am feeling better. In Butte there wasn't much to cook with. No vegetables except what was freighted in, and Deadwood was the same. Whoever said gold and potatoes don't grow in the same ground was right!

Mother Earp loves animals, especially horses. She keeps a pair out back just to talk to, and it's funny to watch them with her. They're trained so well they're almost like dogs, except that she said that as soon as you start thinking a horse is a dog, it'll kill you. Then she laughed and hugged one of them and said: "Don't even think of it, you big brute!"

I never met a woman quite like her. She's so determined I'm always waiting for Father Earp to get mad, but he never does, just dotes on her. He told me that when she was young she could ride anything on four feet, so it's easy to see where my husband and his brothers get their knack with horses.

The old folks are going away for a week, so me and my old man are going to a dance tomorrow night. I guess I won't be able to dance much, but it should be fun anyhow. His folks don't believe in dancing, being strict Methodists, but like I wrote, they have been very kind to me and I am not as homesick as I was. Morgan keeps planning to send me back for a visit, but money is tight, and he worries that I'll take sick and him not around.

I don't know if the poppy seeds I'm sending will grow where you are, but you might try. When they bloom here, it looks like whole hills and valleys are on fire. I wish I could think of a better way to write it, but I don't have the words.

Love from your sister,
Louisa Houston Earp

Temescal, July 19, 1880
Dear Sister Agnes:

"My husband starts for Arizona in the morning. I am going to stay here for the present with his parents. They do not want me to go, and I do not want to go.

"We have had ripe peaches, watermelons, and green corn for a month, and no rain for four months.

"The thermometer has not been above 80 for a month, and most of the time at 65 or 70. Nights are very cool. We cannot sleep without a quilt over us.

"This is written so badly I don't think you can read it very well. I have no news to write at present, so I will have to close. Give my love to all.

Louisa Houston Earp"

Temescal, August 30, 1880
Dear Sister Agnes:

"I am very glad to hear from you and to hear that you are well and that mother's health is improving. My health is about the same. I thought at first I was improving fast, but think I'm at a standstill as I have had the rheumatism a great deal lately. It has become second nature to me to be sick. If I were well, I would not know myself. I think I should run around so much that I would make myself sick, so it is about the same."

My husband wrote from Arizona that it has rained there for sixty days and the whole country is flooded. As I write from here, I look out on trees, flowers, a paradise, but as you know, it's useless for me to attempt to describe anything. How I wish I could! It's irksome not to be able to communicate the way I want. What do people do with the thoughts and feelings they carry inside? The ones they can't express?

I will close for now — and send along this poem.

> **"There's not a joy this world can give
>   like that it takes away.**
> **When the early thoughts decline in
>   feelings dwell decay.**
> **'Tis not on youth's smooth cheek the
>   blush alone which fades so fast.**
> **But the tender bloom of heart is gone
>   ere youth itself is past."**

Your loving sister,
Louisa Houston Earp

Tombstone, Arizona Territory, December, 1880
Dear Sister Agnes:

So you know where I am, I joined my husband here a few weeks ago. Once again, all the younger Earps are together, which is pleasant as we wives can cook and sew and shop when our husbands are busy or out of town as they often are.

This place is not like California, though the climate is pleasant and flowers grow even in winter. There is a great deal of political trouble, as with any mining town I guess, but life in Temescal was peaceful compared to here. I can't describe it, but am sending a copy of the newspaper for you to read.

I went to the Mexican camp today to buy a bird. Almost every family here has at least a mockingbird or a parrot, which the Mexicans bring up from Mexico. The singing birds cost from five to twenty dollars, and Morgan, who knew I wanted one, told me to go and pick whichever I liked.

I bought a little yellow bird that so far hasn't sung. I put his cage in the window that looks out on the street and across the desert to the Dragoon Mountains, and maybe there is too much for him to take in.

Morgan says he'll get used to everything. I thought maybe I should let him go, but Morgan wouldn't let me. He said a hawk would get it before it flew half a mile, and I guess that's so. Some things are born in cages and can never get out, no matter what.

In this part of the country where the weather is mild and the mountains stand out so clear against the sky, it is easy to think that you could fly if you wanted to. Sometimes I almost believe it myself, which is funny when I think of it. Me and my swollen joints and the pain that never quite leaves me.

Well, enough. Please write soon.

With love from your sister,
Louisa Houston Earp

Tombstone, Arizona Territory, July, 1881

Dear Agnes:

The most pitiful thing to see is a marriage between people who don't suit. These past months it seems that everyone is fighting — in the town and in the house.

The town situation is very dangerous. We wives aren't allowed to go out alone for fear something will happen, and, just like anything caged too long, we've started bickering — mostly Mattie, Wyatt's wife, and Allie who won't put up with what she thinks is nonsense.

Mattie's been complaining because Wyatt has been gone most of the time, and people have been talking about his interest in a woman who came to town with an acting troupe and is now engaged to our sheriff. I've seen her, and she's much prettier than Mattie, and doesn't look like she ever whined or complained a day in her life. That's all Mattie does — to Wyatt and to the rest of us when he's gone. It does wear on a person, especially coming out of Mattie who, to be honest, isn't very smart and keeps repeating herself. The other day it got to Allie who told her to stop being a baby and find something to do.

"Treat him nice, you fool," she told her.

"Maybe he'd come home more often if you shut your mouth and used what the Lord gave you."

Then Mattie got mad, she does have a temper, and ran out and slammed the door, and Allie stood there shaking her head. "Poor critter. Hasn't got a lick of sense. I never could tell what Wyatt saw in her."

"She wants so hard," I said.

Allie has a way of summing everything up. "There's a loser in every race, and she's it."

Then there's Morgan's friend Doctor Holliday who's here in Tombstone, too, but without his wife who refused to stay here with him, which sometimes I think was very smart. She did come for a visit after the fire — half the town burned not long ago, but we weren't in any danger —and talked me into going to Doc to get a tooth fixed.

While he worked he went on and on about Kate thinking she was too good to live in Tombstone, and who did she think she was when she'd been a whore and everybody knew it.

Well, when he finished, I told him I thought Kate was a lady, and that he'd have to look a long time before he found another like her, especially here.

He has odd-colored, blue-gray eyes, and he looked at me like he could see through me. "You don't understand. How could I explain that she was a whore?"

I laughed in his face. Don't know where I got the courage. "Nobody here would care," I told him. "Besides, there's women who're just as bad but won't admit it."

Well, we know it's true. We know women who've married badly just so they wouldn't starve, and women who covet men not their husband, and what is that called? But Doc is the kind of man who won't ever understand, not like Morgan — or his brothers, either. Doc wants everything perfect. Morgan takes things as they come. It hasn't been easy with me sick, but he's stayed close and for that I'm grateful.

I'm writing all this out of the need to talk — to straighten out my head. But doesn't it seem like a lot of the world's troubles start with what goes on between a man and woman? Or between folks who can't talk? It does to me.

I hope to be able to go and get some cactuses in a few weeks. It's been raining hard and Morgan has been gone, so there's not been anyone to take me.

Please send my love to everyone, and keep much for yourself.

Louisa Houston Earp

Tombstone, September 4, 1881
Dear Sister Agnes:

"I am very glad you are well and happy. I am about as usual. I went out to the mountains and stayed a week, but I did not get any cactuses. There were none like I wanted to get.

"I will send you a piece of California Liveforever that my sister-in-law sent me . . . also some sprouts of verbena and bergamot . . . I got them through the mail in a small box and will send them to you the same way. If they are not delayed, they will grow I think.

"Our city is in a big excitement. The Indians are on the warpath all around us and have killed a great many people . . . Some here are terribly afraid, but I think the place is too large to be taken easily, and there are three forts within forty and fifty miles of Tombstone. The news only came in last night about the Indians, but, of course, it is exaggerated, at least we all hope so.

"I remain as ever your affectionate sister,
Louisa Houston

"P.S. I will send you a piece of my hair in this, and a piece for Olive."

Tombstone, A. T. November, 1881
Dear Sister:

There has been much trouble here involving my husband and his brothers and a bunch of outlaws who have been running wild and terrorizing the county for too long.

Three of them were killed in a street fight, and my husband was wounded, shot through his shoulders, but he is recovering. He wanted me to go to California to stay with his parents, but I think it best to stay here with him. We have moved to the Cosmopolitan Hotel so no one of the outlaws can just walk in on us, as happened once at home. It is hard being so unsettled, not knowing what will happen next or to whom.

Allie, Bessie, and I are making a quilt to pass the time. I believe it is called "Flower Garden." Do you quilt? If you would like some pieces I can send them.

I wish we had not come here. It is an evil place and I doubt it will ever be any different.

From your sister,
Louisa Houston Earp

Tombstone, Arizona Territory, February 4, 1882
Dear Sister Kate:

It is quite impossible to write all the trouble and anxiety we have had. Morgan's brother, Virgil, was shot over a month ago and was not expected to recover, though now it appears that he is on the mend.

Allie is almost worn out from nursing him but won't hear of one of us taking her place. It is doubtful that he will ever use his arm again, though Allie says as long as he has at least one arm to hold her with, she won't complain.

He was ambushed on the street, by those same outlaws I wrote about before, and we are all afraid, for it could happen again any time to any of us. Life hangs by a thread. We must make the most of every moment, for there may not be another.

Your loving sister,
Louisa Houston Earp

Colton, California, September, 1882
Dear Sister:

It is many months since I wrote. The idea of reliving a nightmare, of having to explain actions that are unexplainable, defeated me.

My husband was murdered in Tombstone in March, shot in the back by one of those outlaws who had been causing all the trouble. He went so fast there was barely time for me to say good bye. Thinking back, our life together was only a short time, too. Still, what we had was sweet. He was a good man and a good husband, and I miss him as if some part of me was cut out. There are still days when I expect him to come into the room or be sitting at the table. And then memory comes back, and I think I am the loneliest person in the world.

Doc Holliday went crazy the night they shot my husband. He ran through town looking for Frank Stillwell, who everybody suspected, and when he couldn't find him he came to the hotel with a suit in his hands.

"Morg and I had a pact," he said, trying to explain. "Whoever went first would wear the other's clothes. I always figured it'd be me. He was a good friend, and I'll miss him."

The next day we left for California, as sorrowful a group as ever was — Allie and Virgil with his useless arm, mourning his brother, Jim and Bessie Earp, their faces weary, Mattie, Wyatt, and me — a widow not able to believe what had happened.

We went by wagon to Contention where we got on the train, and Doc Holliday and some of our friends rode with us, as much to protect as to say a last farewell. I'll never forget the look on Doc's face as he said good bye to me. It was like a mask, angry and sad at the same time.

"We'll get them," he said. "Wyatt and I will get every damn' one of them."

"It won't bring him back," I answered.

"It won't, but they'll get what they asked for." He hugged me, and I started to cry and couldn't stop, though I tried so hard to be brave.

Later we heard that he and Wyatt killed Stillwell at the station in Tucson and then took off in search of the rest of the gang, but Wyatt hasn't been home yet, so I can't really say.

The rest of us are still here at Mother and Father Earp's, still grieving, but each day is a little better than the last. Only Mattie is fussing, as usual. She wants to leave because she says the old folks don't like her. Can't say as I blame them. She's a chore to live with, and it's not her husband who's dead!

What am I going to do? It's hard to say. I am not thinking clearly, if I ever did. Until you hear different, you can write me at this address.

Know that I love you all.

Your sister,
Louisa Houston Earp

Los Angeles, California, February 3, 1886
Dear Sister Kate:

"After my long neglect, I at last seat myself to write a few lines. I am in very good health at present and hope this will find you the same. . . .

"I was married on New Year's Eve . . . and will send Mama some of the wedding cake. I think there will be a little for all of you. . . .

"I have lived in Los Angeles since last April. It is a beautiful place — the oranges are just ripe now and most of the roses and lilies are in bloom.

"I shall not write very much this time. My husband writes Papa and Mama a letter also.

"With my best love to all I will close hoping to hear from you very soon.

"From your affectionate sister Louisa Peters"

Los Angeles, January 3, 1886
Mrs. Agnes Cebell:

"When you read the signature of this letter, you will certainly wonder by what right a stranger addresses these lines to you, but having studied the contents it will prove that, as the rulings of an Almighty having favored me, I have won the hand and heart of your dear sister Louisa. I am since December 31, 1885, her true and lawful husband. Consequently your brother-in-law and as such I beg you to hold good will towards me. . . .

"Your brother, Gustav H. Peters"

Long Beach, California, Sept. 6, 1894
Mrs. Agnes Cebell
Dear Madam:

"Although a stranger allow me to address you as your brother-in-law . . . I, Henry G. Peters, married your sister Louisa on the 31st of December, 1884 in Los Angeles through the Rev. G. Dorsey, Minister of the Gospel. We have been very happy during our married life, which ended on the 12th June, 1894. My dear Lou was attacked with Sciatic Rheumatism for the last three years, to which Dropsy added itself and ended her sufferings.

"I have written to father and mother asking their blessing, but never received a reply. . . .

"If this letter reaches you, please answer it immediately. . . .

      "Best wishes from your brother-in-law.
      G.H. Peters"

Fiddle Case

A True Story

On the Santa Fé Trail, on the 1st of August, 1858, Jerusha Stiles gave birth to a daughter. The wagon train had laid over, not out of consideration for her, but because the night before Indians had run off a hundred head of horses that were being driven to Fort Union.

Wagon Master Tobias Johns, who hadn't wanted a woman in Jerusha's condition along, but who'd given in when faced with the determination of her and her husband, Sam, smiled, hearing the cry of the newborn. At least that much was going well.

In Fort Leavenworth, Jerusha had assured him she would be no bother, and he, unused to such a forthright discussion with a woman, had given in with the comment: "See that you aren't, Missus Stiles." And to Sam: "It's your responsibility. We leave in two days. Waiting for that government train and their horses has made us late starting already."

True to her word, Jerusha had been no trouble, just the opposite in fact. She'd been a comfort to the McGinnis family when their youngest son had gotten run over and was buried deep under the ruts of the trail. She'd been the first to befriend Amelia and Notion, the freed black couple traveling with Joshua and Elizabeth Edwards, and the first to discover that Amelia, called Meelie, had a knowledge of medicine that had already come in handy. Meelie had a cure for everything from routine insect bites to stomach upset, and she was a skilled midwife who'd been with Jerusha since before dawn. Silently Tobias tipped his hat in the direction of the Stiles' wagon, and continued his reconnaissance.

It was noon. Around him the prairie shimmered in the heat until it seemed the land was breathing, as if it were alive and all of them perched on its golden back. He smiled at his notion as he did every time he allowed himself to picture it — earth as a huge beast, and he and his wagons, the horses, cattle, people, nothing more than a bunch of fleas lost in the rippling hide.

And noisy fleas at that, he thought, seeing the children playing hide-and-seek, the women chattering as they hung laundry on the ropes strung between each wagon, a makeshift clothesline the children immediately began to use in their game.

Meelie climbed down from the Stiles' wagon, a bundle of bloody rags in one hand. "Afternoon, Cap'n." She smiled, pleased with the day's work.

"How's Missus Stiles?"

"Right as rain. And she's got a fine baby girl. Just listen to that child yell!"

"Hard not to." His own smile was relieved. Death on the trail, especially in childbirth, tended to cast a pall over the rest. "Tell her I'll look in this evening."

"Yes, suh. I will. When you reckon we'll be pulling out?"

"Not till the soldiers get back. With or without those horses." Standing in his stirrups, he looked out at the horizon, saw nothing but grass, the deep, red ruts of the trail, the narrower trails made by the hoofs of buffalo, the sky a half circle above, its blue dimmed by the fierce sunlight.

For all their sakes, he hoped the searchers hadn't ridden into ambush. There was safety in numbers, particularly here, miles from anything resembling help. Going on without the soldiers, regardless of the fact that some of them were green as grass and hardly able to stay on a horse, was plain asking for trouble. Trouble he didn't need.

Damn the Indians! Without them, his job would be simple. If he had his way, not a one would be left alive. His memories were of the Spirit Lake Massacre, of a young wife and unborn child, his dreams ripped apart like Jenny's belly had been.

Seeing his scowl, the children scattered, and the women turned away, fearful they'd done something wrong. They whispered about the new baby, and about the fierce look on the wagon master's face, glancing over their shoulders at the man on the big buckskin horse circling the camp — the man who held their lives in his hands.

Jerusha looked at the infant, secure in the crook of her arm, and marveled at the fact that she and Sam had produced this black-haired, indignant little person who, although bathed, wrapped, and in her mother's loving care, was loudly demanding attention, food, recognition. No fragile flower, this child. No whimpering nuisance. This girl would make herself known wherever she was. The first, fierce pangs of mother love swelled unexpectedly in Jerusha's throat. She hadn't foreseen this need to protect that was almost the equal of her daughter's more vocal passion.

"My goodness!" she said to Sam. "I think she'll be a singer one day. Musical, just like her daddy!"

All morning, while he had paced outside the wagon, Sam had been reliving the war whoops of the Indians the night before as they galloped in and drove away the horses. It was a sound he hoped never to hear again, but which he knew would remain in his head the rest of his life.

Blindly determined to set out for California, he'd put his family in danger, risked not only himself and Jerusha, but the life of this strident but beautiful child.

"We should have waited," he said. "We should've stayed in town."

Jerusha laughed. "Nonsense. Think what a story she'll have to tell. Born in a wagon with Indians all around."

"But. . . ."

She shook her head. "Life hangs by a thread no matter where you are. There was cholera in

Fort Leavenworth. We couldn't take a chance on that. It's better here for all of us."

She loved the days on the trail — the rhythm of them, the creak of wagons, the steady motion of hoofs, the heat, the dust, the storms that seemed to split heaven and earth and left the air scented with flowers she couldn't name. And she loved the company of the other women, the challenge of cooking over a fire in the middle of the prairie, the pleasure of doing her wash in a clear-running stream, and at night the music of Sam's fiddle, all of the company dancing, even the children who giggled and tripped on their feet to the laughter and applause of their parents.

And now there was a daughter with whom to share her delight, an empty slate upon which she could write the things that mattered. Leaning over, she put a hand on Sam's arm. "We'll all be fine," she whispered. "I'm sure of it. Now tune up your fiddle and give us a hymn."

Outside, Meelie poked the embers of the fire and waited until all evidence of birth had burned to ash, thanking God for an easy time and a healthy baby. Maybe, when they got to California, she and Notion could start a family of their own. Always they'd put it off, unwilling to bring a child into slavery, frightened of the risk of separation. And then Mr. Edwards, in opposition to his slave-owning neighbors, had granted them freedom and the chance to go West. And freedom was precious. As precious as life.

She said another silent prayer, then made her way across the circle formed by the wagons, pushing away the notion that wood, canvas, a few men with rifles and a few courageous women were puny protection against the savages she had seen swooping down like hawks after prey. Sam's music brought her out of her reverie. Lordy, how that man could play!

He sat on the wagon tongue, fiddle tucked under his chin, eyes closed, playing to his daughter and to Jerusha whom he loved even more than his music, although sometimes it was hard to separate the two. She had always been like a song, a melody that stayed with him no matter what he did, a rippling of notes that gave his life meaning and form, even here where the world had no limits, and the horizon kept moving away.

Gradually his daughter's crying subsided, and he bent his head over the strings and played her a gentle lullaby.

It was the next afternoon before the soldiers got back, driving sixty weary horses.

"Damned Injuns split up." Captain Roger Moser was as tired as the horses and looked it, his eyes bloodshot, his face unshaven and streaked with sweat and dust. "There wasn't enough of us to follow both trails, so now we're forty horses short."

"Better that than lose your scalps," Tobias said, subtly congratulating the young officer's

135

good sense. "Let the horses graze a while. To-night bring them inside and set a double watch. We'll head out in the morning."

"No chance of us going after the rest?"

Tobias sighed. "By now those redskins are a hundred miles away and scattered. You'd come back empty- handed . . . if you came back. We're behind schedule as it is. I'm figuring on taking the Cimarron Cut-Off."

Moser looked unhappy. "That's a dry run, isn't it?"

"But not impossible. We'll carry all the water we can."

A cry split the air like a church bell, and Moser winced. "What the hell's that?"

Tobias grinned. "Missus Stiles has what's called by the ladies, a little visitor, and she ain't shut up but once since she got here."

"Jesus!" Moser said.

"Trouble is, now every Injun between us and the Missouri knows just where we are, but I can hardly tell her ma to gag her, can I?"

"Maybe she'll tire herself out," Moser said, so tired himself he thought he would even sleep through the child's crying.

"Don't count on it." No matter how much he groused, Tobias had to admire the kid's spunk with that part of himself he kept hidden, the place he'd sealed off years before. "At least we know she ain't sickly," he said before he rode off toward the Stiles' wagon for a glimpse of mother and child.

Jerusha had always been one of the first to wake and watch the night lift tenuously off the prairie, and this day, the second of her daughter's life, was no different. As the sky lightened and the grass turned from silver to gold, she held the child up to watch.

"See!" she said. "It's another day, and we're going to California, you, me, your daddy, and all the rest, and, oh, isn't it all beautiful?"

The infant, as if she heard, turned her head toward the sun and began to wail, and Meelie made her way across the circle of men, women, and children.

"Lordy, Miz Stiles," she said. "That child's gonna trumpet us all the way to California!"

"Is she all right?" Suddenly frightened, Jerusha turned to the older woman.

"Sure she is! Maybe a touch of the colic, but don't you mind. This little gal's so full of life, nothin's gonna stop her, so don't you fret."

"I've named her Hope," Jerusha said. "Hope for all of us."

Meelie reached out and laid a gentle hand on the baby's head. "It's a fine name. And she's a fine child. Between us, we'll get this baby to California safe and sound."

"You're sure?" Jerusha clutched the wriggling bundle closer.

"I am. Don't doubt it."

Jerusha looked at her new friend, blue eyes meeting brown. "I don't, Meelie," she said. "Not with you along."

After all, there was no difference between them, only the color of the skin that lay over hearts that were full of loving and full of knowledge of what it meant to stick together, their feet planted firmly, their eyes on the miles that lay in front of them like a distant mirage.

The Cimarron Cut-Off headed Southwest — dry plains without water, an expanse of ground that rose and fell in a sameness that was harshly beautiful, that tore, aching, into the gut, the bone, the eyes of those who made their painful way across. Low grass, cacti, dry streambeds, and always drifting herds of buffalo, antelope flashing white rumps, bands of horses running wild as the wind that never stopped whipping at the canvas wagon tops, at faces dried into wrinkles and covered with sand blown a thousand miles.

Looking out from her seat inside the wagon, Jerusha thought she'd never seen any place so forlorn, as if it had been forgotten by God and man. Behind her she could see the rest of the train moving slowly through a cloud of dust, and she wondered if the water would hold out, if she herself had the strength to keep on. Her whole body ached, and her eyes burned, as much from lack of sleep as from trail dust. How long had it been since she'd slept more than a few hours, before Hope's angry crying awakened her?

Maybe she had been wrong to insist on leaving

Fort Leavenworth. If so, it was too late to change her mind. Too late to do anything but what she was doing, soothing, rocking, desperately attempting to quiet not only the baby but her own misery.

She looked down at Hope's flushed face. "Please," she whispered. "Please stop it."

Strangely, Hope's wail subsided into a series of hiccups. She stiffened for a moment as if surprised, then closed her eyes and seemed to sleep.

Jerusha laid her down, then poked her head out the front of the canvas. "She's asleep."

Sam turned to smile at her. "Get some rest yourself, why don't you?"

"I'd as soon sit up here with you a while," she said, crawling through beside him.

"And I'll be glad of your company." If the truth was told, although he loved his new daughter, Sam had missed his wife.

"It won't always be like this." She laid a hand on his arm. "I guess to her the world's a pretty frightening place. So big. So . . ." — she looked around at the rolling plain — "so empty," she finished, with something like despair in her voice. Suddenly she was stricken with homesickness, with the need to see the woods of her childhood, the creek that rushed at the foot of the hill, and, if not the woods, at least a single tree, leaf-covered, green, dancing.

She wrapped her arms around herself. "How much longer?"

Sam shrugged. "Hard to say. Maybe a week,

139

but we should see the mountains before that. You're not worried, are you?"

A week! It seemed like a year, and her struggling with a cranky baby, dirty diapers, and not enough water to spare for the washing of them.

"No," she said in a whisper. "No. I'm not worried. Just tired." She shut her eyes against the glare of the sun, the sight of the plains bronzed by summer heat, marked by the wheels of a thousand wagons, the dragging feet of armies of the hopeful.

The women were gathering buffalo chips for the cooking fires. She could hear their voices clearly, some laughing, some filled with disgust at the necessity to use chips for fuel.

"In all my born days, I never figured on this." That was Eliza Edwards, plantation born, unused to dirty hands or the doing of chores.

And then Meelie. "It's just chewed up grass, Miz Edwards. You go sit down. I'll git enough for both of us."

Jerusha picked herself up out of the narrow bed at the side of the wagon. She must have slept the afternoon away. Miraculously, so had Hope. A glance at the basket showed her, eyes closed, peaceful.

"Let her sleep," Jerusha prayed. "Just a little bit longer." Just long enough so that she could join the women, see to dinner without interruption.

There was grit in her mouth and on her face,

and she thought how good it would be to bathe in a stream, to be clean all over, hair washed, fingernails white. But she was only making herself miserable, she decided, smoothing her hair and running her hands over her face to remove the worst of the dirt. Everyone was in the same shape, hot, grimy, sparing all the water for the animals.

Summoning a smile, she climbed out, picked up a bucket, and joined the rest.

"So she finally made up her mind to sleep," Meelie said in greeting.

"And I even got a nap."

Meelie lifted her head and stood listening. "Makes you remember . . . 'cept for us, this country's quiet as the first day of creation."

Aside from the bustle of camp, the braying of mules, the high, shrill laughter of children, the land around them was wrapped in a silence that had been undisturbed for centuries, a silence broken only by the sound of moving buffalo, an occasional bird, the long breath of wind.

Jerusha shivered, and Meelie eyed her with suspicion. "You all right? You ain't sickenin' with something?"

"I'm fine. A goose on my grave, as my mother used to say."

"You just feelin' blue 'cause you ain't slept but a wink since that child came. Go on back and sit. I'll bring enough of these here flat cakes to git everybody's supper."

In spite of herself, Jerusha laughed. "Really,"

she said, "I'm fine. It's good to be outside, even if there isn't anything to see. Not even a tree."

"Lots to see. You just got to look," came the response. "The trouble is, most folks don't bother."

"I guess." Jerusha bent and scooped up a handful of dry chips. "Still, it's a lonesome place, and I'll be glad when we're across."

"Soon enough, honey." Meelie's voice was dark and soothing. "Soon enough."

But it wasn't. When Jerusha and Sam climbed into the wagon a few minutes later, Hope lay cold and still, not breathing.

Jerusha felt her heart splinter into a thousand pieces like a mirror dropped upon stone, and the cry that she made was muted by terror, and by the pain that stopped her throat.

Together she and Sam knelt by the basket. Jerusha lifted the limp body and held it close, as if she could will life and warmth back into the child's pale face and dangling limbs, give back the voice that had held an entire wagon train spellbound.

"No," she whispered. "No!"

Beside her, Sam bent his head and wept the tears she couldn't summon, wept without shame for all of them, his arms around his wife's shoulders in what he knew was useless comfort.

Neither could ever remember how long they knelt, a pageant of grief held motionless, before Jerusha lifted her head, her eyes crazed.

"I won't bury her here. I won't. Not where there's nothing. Not under this damned trail." In her head she saw it, the ruts driven deep into the ground, bodies buried beneath the red dirt, bodies turned to dust and bone that, in one year or twenty, would rise to the surface and be taken by coyotes or wolves or whatever creatures haunted this emptiness. "I won't," she repeated, still with the wildness in her eyes. "You have to help me, Sam."

"How?" Bewildered, he spoke around his own pain.

"We'll just say she's asleep. She is, you know. Just look at her, the darling. Sound asleep."

"Jerusha. . . ."

"No," she said sternly. "Let her be until we're out of this place. Until we're where we can leave her safe."

In the face of her hysteria, he forced himself to be calm, summoning courage from a source he hadn't known was there. "I'll take care of you both, sweetheart. I'll. . . ." He stopped and looked around the cluttered interior for something, anything that would distract her, and saw his fiddle case lying empty, the fiddle where he'd left it on top of a trunk.

When he spoke again, his hands wove the spaces between his words, and she watched them, hypnotized. "I'll make her a bed in the fiddle case. She'll just fit, and she'll like it there. I know she will. Now find something to wrap her in and help me."

But Jerusha was singing, not to him, but to the

143

child, a mournful lullaby, and she seemed not to have heard him.

"Jerusha. . . ." He took her arm and felt it trembling, and in that moment accepted the burden that was laid on him — his wife's madness, the death of his only child, and the optimism of the hundred or more people around the cooking fires, keeping watch, laughing, talking about their futures, whatever they would be.

He found a shawl and carefully took the still body from Jerusha's arms, and wrapped it in an embroidery of birds and butterflies, flowers and leaves, a piece of cloth made by some forgotten ancestor for a reason then unknown.

"We'll put her here," he said, his voice cracking no matter how he tried to steady it. "We'll put her where the music is."

"Play something."

"Later."

"No," she said fiercely. "Play now. We can't tell them. They'll make us leave her. Play now like everything is the same."

Stiffly she climbed out of the wagon, and Sam followed, his fiddle tucked under one arm. They were greeted with smiles and kind words.

"How's little Hope?"

"She's stopped crying. A blessing for you."

Jerusha met the questions with a sculpted face. "Thank you. Yes, she's sleeping, poor lamb."

And now, Tobias thought, *we can all sleep at night,* although the sight of Jerusha's eyes and the shadows beneath them caught his attention. *Was she sickening of cholera, on the verge of infecting his entire train? Had they come this far only to be wiped out, as so many had been because of some unseen evil carried on the wind?* He paused by the wagon and tipped his hat, manners taught him by his mother, that fierce old woman who believed in politeness regardless of circumstance.

"You're all right, Missus Stiles?"

"Certainly," she said, and looked down at her hands, gripped together to keep them from shaking. "Thank you," she added as an after-thought, and refused to meet his eyes.

"Missus Stiles. . . ." He broke off, feeling foolish.

"Yes?"

"You'll tell me if anything is wrong, I hope."

She caught her lower lip in her teeth and stood still as a hunted rabbit. Then she said: "I think I can manage, thank you just the same."

It wasn't the answer he'd expected or wanted, but he felt himself dismissed. "That's good, then." He stood beside her like a schoolboy, waiting, for what he couldn't tell.

And then Sam came out of the wagon, his fiddle carried carefully in his hands.

Tobias was relieved. Music meant distraction from the stress of the trail, from the water barrels that were thick with slime and algae, a mess that only the animals drank with relish. "Music to-night?" he asked.

Sam's long fingers caressed the shape of the fiddle as if he were blind. He plucked at the

145

strings one at a time, then nodded slowly. "I'll play. For all of us." Then his mouth snapped shut in a straight line that seemed, to Tobias, to be a grimace of pain. But why? He put a hand on Sam's shoulder.

"Another couple days should see us out of here. Tell your wife, and play happy."

Oh, yes. Play happy. And Hope dead, his wife turned stranger, her face carved out of stone. How long would it be before the stench of death betrayed their ghastly secret? He put his bow to the strings and bent his head to hide his tears.

That night the immense silence of the plain echoed with music wrenched from his heart. No one danced. Instead, they sat listening as their lives spun out transformed into sound that seemed not to be sound at all but was joy and sorrow made tangible.

That night, Meelie, in recognition of the grandmother she had never known — the woman whose daughter had been snatched away from her and sold, to be swallowed up in the dark maw of cotton and cane fields — that night, Meelie turned to Notion who lay beside her and pulled him close. "Let's us be happy in this world," she whispered. "Let's us give thanks."

That night, Tobias remembered his Jennie with the familiar, stabbing pain, and then thought, with equal longing of Flavia, the trader's daughter in Santa Fé — Flavia, whose laughter was like the notes of Sam's fiddle.

That night, Roger Moser, guarding his horse

herd, wondered how the squalling baby could sleep through such a racket.

And hidden in an arroyo, the Kiowa war party that had been tracking the wagons for two days, listened to the spirit voice, and each man was filled with fear. By morning they were gone, sixteen shadows unnoticed in the dance of heat waves above the plain.

That night, Sam and Jerusha lay awake listening to the moan of the wind in the canvas wagon top, listening for a sound from the child who lay soundless, wrapped in a flowered shawl in the old leather fiddle case. Neither of them spoke.

They went on. A day passed, then two, and on the evening of the third day, like a mirage, a mountain rose in the distance, splitting the horizon in half. Around the fires that night there was gaiety and joking, laughter that spilled out like water from parched throats.

"Nearly there!"

"We done it!"

"Praise the Lord!"

And in the wagon Jerusha sat, her arms wrapped around herself. Soon, too soon, she would lay her daughter in the earth and be forced to go on with the mark of her loss branded forever on her heart.

Sam came to the rear of the wagon. "Jerusha. Come out."

"No."

"Please."

"I'm staying with her. Tell them I'm sick. Tell them anything you want."

Shoulders sagging, he turned away.

"Play for us again tonight, Mister Stiles?" Meelie stood in his path, eyes sparkling. "Seems we ought to celebrate with a dance, and those mountains so close."

He stared at her in silence a moment. Then he said: "Is that all anybody can think about? Dancing?"

She stared back, hearing the pain behind his words, and put out a hand. "I don't mean to pry, but if somethin's wrong, best tell me. Maybe I can help."

It was the touch of her hand, strong and warm, that did him in. But when he tried to speak, a sob choked him. "The baby. . . ."

She gripped him harder. "Oh, Lord! It's not the cholera, Mister Stiles. Say it ain't."

He shook his head.

She turned away and climbed quickly into the wagon, peering through the darkness to where Jerusha sat motionless. "What's wrong, honey?"

Her arms still around herself, Jerusha began to rock back and forth. "Dead," she said tonelessly. "Dead, dead."

"Oh, sweet Jesus!" Meelie knelt beside her. "And you never said. Jist sat here, takin' it on yourself and like to lost your mind."

"I couldn't . . . leave her out here. In this place."

"I know, honey. I know it's hard." Meelie

looked around and caught sight of Hope lying in the fiddle case, her face shimmering in the darkness, and something, she never knew what, caught at her, made her breath come short. Her next words rang out like the peal of a bell. "Lord a mercy, honey, this baby ain't dead!"

"Don't touch her!" Jerusha stood up and moved between them.

"Now, you listen. Get me some hot water and a tub, and do it quick. This baby's jist sleepin'. Maybe talkin' to the angels and scarin' you half to death. But she ain't dead, and that's a promise. Jist don't go faintin' on me," she added, seeing Jerusha unsteady from shock. "Go, do what I said."

"I can't."

Meelie took the limp body in her arms and stood, and she looked, to Jerusha, like a warrior, like one of the fierce-faced Indians she'd seen riding toward the wagons.

"Don't do this!" she screamed. "She's dead, can't you see?"

"I can see she's got breath, and you actin' like a crazy woman. Now go, do what I told you, honey, and we'll have her screechin' again in no time."

Carefully, the baby close against her breast, Meelie climbed out of the wagon. To Sam she said: "Now don't waste time askin' me questions. Jist help your wife get me a tub of water. This baby's alive." Then she made her way to her own wagon, crooning under her breath.

The women followed her, curious and afraid.

"What happened?"

"Is she all right?"

"Is she dead?"

"She's gonna be fine. Jist give her and me some room."

Seeing Notion, Mellie said: "Take her while I get ready."

Without a word, he held out his arms and took her, wondering if even his wife, whom he'd seen work miracles, could help. "Poor mite," he said, looking down on the pale face and colorless lips. "Poor, helpless little thing." Then he began to sing in a rich baritone, a song so old he couldn't say where he'd learned it, a song with its roots in Africa transplanted to the cotton fields of Georgia, as mournful as those who had given it words.

Meelie hummed along under her breath as she collected the herbs she wanted, her unconscious harmony turning the simple tune into a prayer.

The water in the tub that Sam and Jerusha brought was hot but green with slime, and at the thought of plunging her daughter into it, Jerusha turned away, biting her lip.

"It's all we could find. It . . . it won't hurt, will it?" Sam asked, wondering as he did what possible difference it could make.

"She won't know," Meelie answered. "And if she did, she wouldn't care."

Gently she took Hope from Notion and unwrapped her, giving the shawl back to Sam who stood with an arm around Jerusha. Then, stooping, she lowered the baby into the water.

No one moved. It seemed that they all held their breath, afraid to break what seemed to be a spell, and around them even the land went quiet, without wind or the flight of birds.

After a long while Meelie drew the child out and onto her lap. The oil she rubbed into the tiny body was sweet-scented, and, as her strong dark hands moved slowly over the white skin, she began again to hum.

And then Hope took a breath and yawned, clenching her fists. Slowly she opened her eyes and stared up at her rescuer.

"Magic," Mary McGinnis said, wishing that somehow the same could have been done for her Charley, buried now in a spot no one could ever find.

Eliza, who had never rid herself of prejudice and superstition, whispered: "Voodoo."

"No, ma'am." Meelie smiled down at Hope. "Jist common sense. Some babies don't know where they belong, but she'll be fine enough now with her mama."

Tears streamed down Jerusha's cheeks as she reached out her arms, tears fueled by joy and the terror of what she might have done had she not been so determined.

"How can I thank you? How can I tell you?" she said through quivering lips.

Meelie's smile enveloped them all with its warmth and genuine happiness. "You can go on back and give her something to eat. Reckon she's hungry after all she's been through."

"We might have killed her." Sam's face was white. "My God, Meelie, how did you know?"

She puzzled over it frowning, rubbing the last of the oil into her hands. "I'm not sure, to tell the truth. 'Cept she smelled so sweet. Like some kind of flower. Death smells different. Or maybe the Lord told me. Whispered in my ear that He didn't want that baby back yet. Maybe there's something she's gotta do. And you got to keep her safe so she can do it."

Keep her safe, Sam thought. For the rest of his days he'd think of that precious life sealed up in darkness under the dirt of the trail. If it hadn't been for Jerusha and her stubborn refusal. . . . He shook his head to drive out the horror.

Tobias stopped beside him, wiping his face on his sleeve. "My, God, man! I've seen some peculiar things in my day, but this! I'm glad for you. And for your missus. It could have been different." It would have been, if he'd known, he thought, but didn't say. He'd have been guilty of murder whether he knew it or not, insisting on burying for fear of sickness.

Responsibility, all the miles he'd traveled, sat hard on him in that moment. He was tired of making decisions for his flock, of the sameness of the trail, the threat of attack, of his own night-mares. It would be good to put down roots, sleep under a roof with a woman beside him — a comfortable woman who shared his thoughts, eased his body, laughed like the cooing of doves. Life was short. And precarious. He'd put in enough years out here where any breath could be his last, and where, more often than not, death and sorrow rode alongside the wagons.

He jammed his hat back on his head. "We'll all remember this day, Sam. Now go see your family."

Jerusha was nursing Hope. When she looked up, her eyes were shining and her cheeks were stained pink. "The Lord must have whispered to me, too," she said. "Only I didn't know it. But I must've listened."

He thought, perhaps, there was a bond between mother and child that was stronger even than that between husband and wife, a communion of blood and heartbeat that was never entirely disrupted, and for a moment he was jealous, an outsider looking upon perfection.

Slowly, so slowly it was almost imperceptible, the sun slid behind the mountains, sending one last ray of light across the plain and into the camp. Against it, Sam stood in silhouette, hesitant, lonely, and Jerusha, her instincts sharpened by experience, tasted his bitterness as if it were her own.

He was hers. As much as the child at her breast, they belonged to one another — a family — bound together by near tragedy, by moments of rapture and terror.

"Sit with us," she said. "And hold me, love. I've been alone too long."

Borderlands

Lucas Todd had come to New Mexico to die, or, if blessed with luck, to recuperate from the tuberculosis that had with no warning struck him down.

At the station, his mother wept and cautiously kissed him on both cheeks. "Write us," she whispered. "Tell us how you are. And where."

He promised, returned her hug, then shook hands with his father who had been waiting for the day when Lucas would join him in the bank, only to see his hopes snatched away.

Lucas hadn't wanted to go into the bank, but then he hadn't planned on dying as a way out, either. All his life he'd wanted to paint, much to his father's annoyance. Now, given the chance, he found himself lost in self-pity. As he looked out the train window and watched the world spreading out on all sides, he recognized that he, by contrast, was small, reduced to a frail structure of skin, bone, and labored breath, a poor excuse of a man who had once possessed a dream.

Although he hoped to be able to avoid company and the resulting small talk, those hopes were dashed when he was seated in the dining car with two other men, both in such robust good health that he immediately felt inferior.

"Good evening!" The older of the two, a man in his fifties with a sweeping mustache flecked with gray, leaned toward him across the table. "I am Herman Lubitsch, and this is Arthur Rollins. You may call me Lubitsch. Never have I liked the name Herman." Then he smiled, an enormous smile that revealed a space between two upper teeth.

Lucas cleared his throat. "Lucas Todd," he said.

Lubitsch leaned on his elbows. "And what do you do here on this train, Mister Todd?"

He managed a faint smile to cover his annoyance. "Seeing the country."

"It's bigger than you could have imagined, no?"

"Yes," Lucas said, wishing he could disappear.

Lubitsch took no notice, but gestured out the window at the sunset that was turning the plains to shades of purple and gold. "Incredible. The light. The colors. The . . ." — he searched for the right words, rolling his eyes — "the mystery of emptiness. Like sorrow not quite remembered but carried in the blood."

Startled, Lucas stared at him. Who was this person to speak of color and sorrow in the same breath? "Who are you?" he asked.

The older man smiled again, that gap-toothed, all-embracing expression of internal joy. "Lubitsch!" He almost sang the name. "Painter. Adventurer. Poor man and seeker of unmapped places. Fisherman of lost hearts."

Madman, Lucas added silently, but was cut off in his thought by Rollins who had been enjoying the performance.

"Actually," he put in with characteristic dryness, "actually, we're on a magazine assignment. Lubitsch is an illustrator, and I'm supposed to write about New Mexico and the crisis on the border. It'll be an adventure all right, especially considering the company."

"Crisis?" Lucas asked, feeling even more alien.

"With Mexico, man! Don't you read the papers? Don't you know that Americans are being murdered for no reason by a bunch of revolutionaries?"

Lubitsch intervened. "Arthur, Arthur, not everyone is as interested as we are. After all, Mexico, what is it but a nation of peasants ruled by despots?"

"And wild men playing soldier. Making raids on our ranches. Killing, mutilating. Look what they did to that train at Santa Ysabel. Killed innocent Americans for no reason at all."

"I don't understand." In spite of himself, Lucas was drawn into the conversation, so far removed from his earlier misery.

"It's a revolution with many heads," Lubitsch said. "And it will never succeed because of that. A body needs only one head, providing it's worthy. Ah! Here's the soup at last!" He tied his napkin around his neck and looked like a large child.

"I guess you've both thought about this,"

Lucas said. "I mean, the danger."

"Danger, danger," Lubitsch mimicked, waving his spoon. "It's everywhere. It walks in our tracks, waits around corners. There's no sense in hiding. Better to go meet it. You should come with us. Take a chance. Life is about risks, not about hiding in cupboards."

Lucas sipped his soup, hearing the older man's words like a staccato telegraph message. What life he had was about to end, a life without accomplishment, without any purpose he could name. He sighed, thinking how he'd wanted to become a painter, and how quickly that notion had been squashed by his parents, two people who had never taken a risk in all their years.

He said: "I wanted to paint once."

"So?"

He shook his head. "My family couldn't understand."

"And now?"

"Now it's too late."

Lubitsch finished his soup and stared across the table with fierce gray eyes. "Is never too late. Now you are here, and you have found me. I am firm believer in fate. You will come with us, and I will see what you can do. I am good teacher." He wiped his mouth with a corner of the napkin. "Better to know, eh?"

In spite of his doubts, Lucas tasted the beginning of excitement. Inside his head a voice was clamoring to be heard, a voice he'd been forced to ignore most of his life. His hand, gripping the spoon, trembled. He said: "I'm dying."

Lubitsch's shaggy eyebrows rose. "So are we all."

"That's not what I meant."

"I know what you meant. You have nothing to lose, and this is good, eh, Arthur?"

Arthur, always the observer, had been watching the drama with fascination. "Lubitsch is right. You're welcome to come along in any case."

It wasn't how he'd planned his last months. He'd seen himself in a hotel room reading, sleeping, gradually coughing up his life until the day when everything turned dark and he was gone, leaving no evidence that he'd ever existed. And that, he realized, had been at the root of his misery.

"All right," he said. "If you can put up with me, I'll come."

"More likely the other way around," Arthur said. "But what the hell!"

"Indeed," Lubitsch said, and beamed as a plate of roast beef was put before him. "Indeed. What the hell?"

"The plan is to go south by horse and wagon," Arthur told him after dinner while Lubitsch was enjoying his cigar. "We want to get a feel for what people are thinking, not just on the border but in the rest of the state."

Lucas's heart fell. "It'll be hard."

Lubitsch glowered over the end of his cigar.

"So? This country, *your* country wa[s] [the same] way. Are you saying you are less [human] people?"

"I already told you. I'm on the [ ]. [If I] can't make it, what happens?"

"We'll worry when we need to, not before. It does no good to worry about possibilities."

The man was overbearing and pompous, Lucas thought, but he was also kind and probably trustworthy. If anything happened to him, he doubted they'd leave him on the trail to die, and, perhaps, out in the desert, he could beat his sickness, thumb his nose at death.

"Are you always right?" he asked with a hint of a smile.

"Mostly." Lubitsch's eyes twinkled.

"And if not, he ignores it," Arthur added.

"I never pictured myself doing anything like this," Lucas said, still trying to imagine what lay ahead. "I mean, I thought. . . ."

"Don't think," Lubitsch advised. "Not yet. For now, just look. Feel what you see. And for now, I go to bed. Tomorrow the adventure begins, my friends."

They watched as he made his way down the aisle, then Lucas said: "We're all crazy."

"No," Arthur corrected. "Just you and me."

Lucas didn't sleep right away, but lay listening to the clacking of wheels, the harshness of his own breath, while outside the plains rose gradually, on their way to the Rockies.

"Crazy," he repeated to himself. "Crazy."

e closed his eyes and slept.

In the morning he saw mountains for the first time and was shaken to the core, not with his own insignificance, but with something that approximated joy, as if his mind and heart had suddenly expanded.

"All the photographs, all the paintings are only that," he said to Lubitsch. "Little things."

"We're not God, you see," came the reply. "A pity, I always thought."

There were the colors — purple, gold, ocher, iron-red, and the faintest hint of spring in the swollen tips of cottonwood trees by the river. And there was the sky, the painted dome of a cathedral ceiling.

Face flushed, Lucas asked: "You will teach me, though? You weren't just being polite last night?"

"It will be my pleasure. And who knows? We might both succeed." Lubitsch spread his hands, palms up. "Always we must try. Otherwise, we have betrayed ourselves."

"I wish I'd known you before."

"You know me now. We meet when it's time."

None of it was real, Lucas decided, but he didn't care. If he was dreaming, it was better than cold reality, and, if not, he'd gotten lucky at last.

They stayed in Albuquerque five days outfitting themselves, buying a wagon and two horses and provisions for the journey. When he wasn't buying boots, blankets, clothes he'd never thought he needed, Lucas wandered through the city, aware in every inch of his being of mountains and desert, of Indians wrapped in bright blankets selling beautifully decorated pottery and jewelry that glittered in the brilliant light, of the Mexicans who chattered in their own language so that he wished he could understand. The whole scene seemed a painting come to life, and his fingers itched with his desire to capture what he saw, no matter how badly.

That he had come here to die was forgotten until he and his new friends took the trail south along the great river and he had his first hemorrhage, handkerchief to his mouth, frustration turning him rigid.

"See," he choked. "See. I'll die here, and you can leave me. Just promise to write my parents."

"Hell," Arthur said. "You're a long way from that yet. Rest easy."

"How do you know?" Lucas looked up at him, desperate and afraid.

"Because I've seen worse," the writer told him. "My own mother died coughing. And I've seen you pitch in and help the last couple days. You'll be fine in the morning."

To his astonishment, when he woke, he was clear-headed and without fever. A glance around showed the mountains he'd come to recognize, the valley rippling with hills of pink sand, and the river, hemmed by reeds and mesquite thickets, humming its way to the Gulf.

161

If he was short of breath, it was because everything around him stirred the voice he'd never acknowledged. It was because, as he watched, the world came slowly to light and life, the river turning from pewter to rose, mirroring the sunrise, and high up, so high they were unidentifiable except for their music, a misshapen V of cranes spattering the sky.

He picked up the sketchbook he'd bought, knowing, as he began, he wouldn't be pleased with the results, and five minutes later he ripped out the page, crumpled it, threw it into the fire beside the blue enamel coffee pot.

"Patience," Arthur said. "Patience."

"Easy for you to say."

Arthur closed the journal he'd been writing in. "What I do is just as hard, maybe harder. You try making pictures out of words and see for yourself."

"I should've stayed in town," Lucas said. "What good am I doing here?"

"Crybaby." Arthur reached for the coffee pot and poured himself a cup. "You are, you know. Just because things aren't going the way you wanted. Because your sketch wasn't a da Vinci. Grow up, man! Success means work. I've spent my life trying to write decent sentences, and Lubitsch practically paints in his sleep. Everything he does or sees gets filed away. Fairy godmothers are a myth, Lucas. If you want hard enough, you have to do the work." He smiled suddenly, and his lean face was oddly gentle.

"Now I'm through preaching. Have some coffee and sit down. You had a bad night."

"Where's Lubitsch?"

"Off drawing birds like Audubon."

"He's good, isn't he?"

"Too good to be wasting his time as an illustrator." Arthur shrugged. "But even he has to eat. And speaking of that, it's time for breakfast." He got up, went to the back of the wagon, and pulled out a slab of bacon and an iron skillet.

Without warning, the scene clicked into focus, a series of lines, straight and curved, of silhouettes against a backdrop of radiant sky. Lucas picked up his pad and began to draw — the wagon with its canvas top, the muscled necks and feathered legs of the horses tethered nearby, Arthur, brown-bearded, his knife flashing in the sunlight, its motion suspended.

Only Lubitsch was missing, but he appeared out of a thicket of reeds, sketchbook under his arm. "So! You're feeling better!" he said to Lucas, then came and peered over his shoulder. "And already immortalizing us."

"Trying to." Lucas attempted to cover up what he'd done, but the older man reached down and took the pad from him.

"Don't be ashamed," he said sternly. "Stand up for what you do, even if it's garbage, which this is not."

"It's rough." Lucas backed away from the subtle praise.

"Stop apologizing. You're not on trial."

"Sorry," Lucas said, then laughed. "It's just I feel like a kid. Helpless all the way around."

"Forget about it. Forget about yourself. The world's more interesting than any one person, even you. And so is breakfast."

In spite of his spell during the night, Lucas was hungry. He couldn't remember when he'd had such an appetite. Maybe, he thought, it was the company, or maybe the air that was clean and sweet, pure as the sandhills, yet carrying, always, the scent of the river. Or, perhaps, it was simply that, for the first time in his life, he had no burden, not even the weight of death grinning at his shoulder. He was like one of Lubitsch's birds that had taken wing and was flying free toward a destination he couldn't see and that was unimportant. It was the flight, itself, that mattered.

Although the nights were cold, the days were warmed by the return of the sun, and along the river farmers prepared their fields for the chiles, squash, corn, and onions that would see them through the year. In the distance were ranches where cattle wandered grazing on grama grass, river reeds, the plumed tops of galleta.

The inhabitants were mixed — Spanish-speaking New Mexicans whose families had been in the same place for centuries, Anglo ranchers seizing the main chance — land and lots of it. Although all were aware of the war on the border, none of them was alarmed.

"You think those greasers'll get up here?" Nate

164

Greening slammed a huge fist on his kitchen table. "Not a chance. This is America, and we protect our own. We've got an army down there, and there's nobody can take us on and win. They think they're gonna take back what belongs to us? Like I said, this is America. We made this country into something, and nobody's coming in here and taking what I busted my ass to build."

Arthur was busy taking notes. Lubitsch and Lucas, having finished the supper Greening had served, sketched by the light of a single lamp.

"You're not worried, then?" Arthur asked.

Greening snorted. "Me and mine will kill anybody that tries to come and take this place. Write that, and say I said it."

In the flickering light his face blurred, became many faces fierce, protective, warrior-like, and Lucas's charcoal slashed across the paper capturing intent.

"*Señores,* what is happening, we don't understand. My family has been here for two hundred years. Under Spain, under Mexico, under America, but always we do what we do, and wish only to be left to do it. What goes on in Mexico, we can't help. We are citizens of this country, and it is good. Better than there. You understand me?"

José Lucero gave Arthur a steady look. "I have no part in any war. My heart, my family are here."

Arthur gave him a bow worthy of a nobleman and returned to the wagon. "Let's go where the action is," he said to the others. "We're not going to find revolutionaries where people are content."

Lubitsch snorted. "A profound statement. And I agree. I'd like to take a bath and sleep in a bed just as a change, you understand. What do you say, Lucas?"

"Now?" Lucas was lost in a painting. For the first time in his life he felt no need to rush, to hide what he was doing, and the intensity of his pleasure took precedence over everything.

Lubitsch, watching him, understood. Once, he had been the same way and could be again if only someone would give him the chance. "Not this minute," he said gently. "Finish what you started. And . . ." — he squinted at the canvas — "you need a little more red in the mountains. Everything in this country has red mixed in."

"Blood," Arthur said.

"Perhaps. Nature is violent."

"So are people. We love our wars and revolutions." Arthur frowned. "Now, how am I going to write that so it's acceptable, I wonder?"

Lubitsch chuckled. "I have faith in you. You'll find a way, and then I'll put it in a picture so everyone will be sure to understand."

Days later they followed the river into La Mesilla, a town of adobe houses, narrow streets, a plaza bordered with elms and with an ornate bandstand in its center.

To the east, the jagged Organ Mountains

caught the light of the setting sun. Across the river, swollen with the first snowmelt, Mexico stretched out like a sleeping lion — tawny, undulant, deceiving in what seemed its emptiness.

They found rooms at a boarding house, put up the horses in the livery, and wandered the narrow *calles,* their presence — strangers — causing talk that rose and fell behind adobe walls and closed gates.

"I feel like a strange disease. A germ under a microscope," Lubitsch remarked as they walked. "Never have I been stared at like this."

"They probably think we're spying," Arthur said. "I'm sure half these people have relatives across the border, and it wouldn't surprise me if some of them made secret visits."

"Is it safe?" Lucas wondered. "Are we?"

Arthur grinned into his beard. "Who can say? After dinner I'll nose around. There must be somebody who'll talk to me."

"I'll come, too," Lucas said, feeling suddenly daring. After all, he was here and charmed by the crooked mud houses with pots of flowers on the windowsills, with chickens squabbling in streets where dark-eyed children played, stared, giggled at the approach of the three strangers. Everything appealed to some part of him that had vanished with his childhood sense of wonder.

"You go," Lubitsch told them. "Take care of each other. I'll go to sleep on a bed."

The town was dark when they left the boarding house. A quarter moon did little to light their way, and the *cantina* they entered had only a few lamps hanging from the ceiling *vigas*. As usual, all conversation stopped until Arthur ordered two beers and they sat down at a rickety table.

"Act natural," he said to Lucas.

"I'm not sure what that is any more." Lucas sipped his beer. "I've turned into somebody else."

And that, Arthur thought, *is true. The kid even looks better, although he still has spells of coughing and sometimes a low fever.* "Just don't turn into a pumpkin," he said. "You'll spoil everything."

Ignoring him, Lucas opened the small sketchbook that now he carried everywhere, and began to draw four men seated at a table in the corner. "Great faces," he murmured.

"And if they object to what you're doing, you'll get knifed either in here or on the way home."

"Be serious."

"I am. And we're about to get a visit from the chief."

Lucas looked up and into the eyes of the man coming toward them, dark eyes that reflected the pale light of the lamps so that it was impossible to read his intentions. "Jesus," he muttered.

"Too late to pray now, kid," Arthur said.

The stranger looked hard at them, particularly at Lucas before he spoke. "*Señores,* you find me and my friends interesting?"

How could a voice so soft, so gentle, sound so

168

menacing? Any words Lucas might have spoken dried in his throat, and he nodded.

"*¿Con su permiso?*" The man stretched out a hand that was hard, callused, uncompromising.

Silently Lucas turned over the tablet and watched as the stranger looked at what he had drawn. Now that he wanted to live, death was, indeed, staring him in the face — death wearing a sombrero that shaded obsidian eyes. He swallowed hard. "You can have it if you want." Besides, if he lived, he could do another. The man's face was printed in his brain.

"*Gracias.*" The sound of the page being torn out sounded loud as a gunshot. He folded it and tucked it in a pocket. "Why are you here, you two?"

Arthur leaned back in his chair. "I'm a writer. Writing about the difficulties on the border. Maybe you can give me your opinion, *señor.*"

The dark face tightened. "I will tell you that no American is honest. That they say one thing and do another. But you won't write that because you are one of them."

"I write facts. I know we may have made a mistake backing Carranza."

"Who would like to see all of you in hell," the stranger interrupted him.

"And Villa?"

"Villa has been betrayed. By everybody. By Americans, by his own. Write that, *señor.* Write how Villa gave the American government what they wanted, and then they turned on him. Write that Villa never forgets treachery. He will make them pay and very soon."

"How?"

The stranger smiled an unpleasant smile. "War, *señores*. The border here is wide, and in this country it is easy to hide an army." Abruptly he turned and walked out into the dark.

Lucas looked at Arthur. "Let's get out of here."

"Can you draw him again?" Arthur, for some reason, was smiling.

"I'll see that face in my sleep. Why?"

"Because, unless I'm mistaken, that was Villa himself."

"You're sure?"

"Yes. Now, like you said, we're leaving. Keep your eyes open. I don't feel like having my throat cut or being one of his prisoners, either."

Lucas forced himself to walk without staggering. In the last weeks he'd gotten an education that he could have done without. Villa's American prisoners had been hanged, trampled to death by running horses, dismembered, all, it seemed, because Villa had lived up to his agreement to return American money and property, and in response President Wilson had given his support to General Carranza, the governor of Chihuahua, Villa's enemy, and a man who wholeheartedly detested the United States.

"That man will never forgive or forget," Arthur said as they stood for a moment in the street. "America has made a mortal enemy out of ignorance."

Around them the town slept. Only the trill of early frogs in the reeds by the river and the sound of a horse trotting south broke the stillness.

Arthur cocked his head to listen, then said: "Tomorrow we're hitting the road."

"Again?"

"We're going to find the war."

Sooner than either man could have predicted, they found it.

West of town the land rose sharply, leveling out on a great, mountain-bordered plain. The wind was in their faces, hard out of the southwest, and Lucas found himself gasping, partly from the force of the wind and partly in astonishment. As far as he could see, the plain was covered with poppies that swayed on delicate stems and made the earth seem to be moving in waves, a petaled, golden sea.

Lubitsch, who was riding in the wagon, boomed in his ear. "Color! Color is everything! Van Gogh said leave out what isn't necessary, and here only color matters. The rest intrudes."

There was this vision, and then there was the insanity of revolution, of men turning against each other, lying, murdering, spilling blood in fields of flowers. A painting danced in Lucas's head — gold and shocking red, the color of blood.

Arthur, who was beside him on the wagon

seat, looked at him. "You all right?"

"Just thinking. About why we . . . I mean why our government has to get mixed up in the whole affair."

"Economics. Politics. And, besides, the Mexicans haven't been good neighbors. We'll have to take a stand sooner or later, instead of being diplomatic and hoping they'll learn to behave and govern themselves. You saw Villa. He's obsessed, and so are the rest."

"Is it possible he's not all bad?" Lucas wondered.

Arthur clucked to the horses. "Sure. When there's no war. But something tells me there's going to be one for a hell of a long time. Don't go feeling sorry, kid. Just look at what is, and you'll be better off."

Lucas looked at the poppies, but once again he saw them dancing in a river of blood.

The wind increased. Sand stung their faces, and the horses lowered their heads and tried to turn away. A rough but well-traveled road led off to the south, and Arthur headed the team down it. "Let's get the hell to a town!" he shouted over the whine of the wind.

The town was Columbus. It was the 8th of March, 1916.

"God help us," Lubitsch said, seeing the scattered houses and Army barracks erected on a flat plain that was unadorned by so much as a single tree. "What can we paint here? We might as well be on the moon."

"Shut the door!" the clerk at the Commercial Hotel shouted at them as they struggled in out of the wind.

"How long?" Lubitsch demanded. "How long will this weather go on?"

"Depends. It's March. Windy all the time. You'll have to share a room. We're full up. What brings you here, anyhow?"

Arthur explained, thinking he was tired of explanations, but the clerk appeared talkative.

"You're in the right place. Villa's around somewheres, or so they say. Kidnapped a ranch foreman just this morning. Poor fellow ain't got a chance. Something's got to be done, but the Army's helpless. They ain't allowed to cross the border to go look."

"How do you know all this?" Arthur asked.

The clerk grinned at him, the lines in his face deepening. "This is a small town. Something happens, we all hear it fast. Besides, the place is full of spies. You want to watch who you talk to and what you say. Everybody's nervous. Can't trust your own neighbor, not if he's a Mex. One minute Villa's over by El Paso, and the next he's down in Palomas ready to jump us. Keep your eyes open and your pistols handy."

"I don't have one," Arthur admitted. "I didn't think. . . ."

"You didn't. That's a fact. Where you from, anyhow?"

"New York."

"That explains it." He pushed the register toward them. "Anybody I should notify in case?"

Lubitsch signed with a flourish, then stuck the pen under the clerk's nose. "Enough! We aren't the fools you think we are."

"Bullets can't tell the difference." He reached behind him for the room key. "Best get yourselves some supper and come right back. It ain't safe to be out at night any more. And you might look up Mister Seese in the room next to you. He says Villa wants to come in and go to Washington, and all this attack talk's rumor." He shook his head. "You folks don't know much about out here. Villa won't come in 'less he's got an army with him. Count on it."

In the late afternoon the wind died and in air as sparkling as glass the Florida mountains seemed close enough to touch.

Looking around, Lubitsch said: "This country . . . it can attach itself to you without your knowing. Then is too late."

"For what?" Lucas asked.

"To leave. To forget what you have seen."

"This town's pretty ugly."

"Man's doing. The rest . . ." — he pointed around them — "the rest is a singing in the heart. I think when we are finished here, I'll find a place to live. And paint. I have for too long denied myself."

"Bravo." Arthur clapped him on the shoulder. "Good for you, you crazy old man!"

And what about me? Lucas wondered. He

174

couldn't stand the idea of locking himself in a room and waiting to die, or of returning home, either. Not after the last weeks. Maybe the land had gotten into him, too, taken possession without his knowing it, like he had fallen in love and was now helpless to do anything but go where that love led.

He said: "Can I come, too? I won't be any trouble."

Lubitsch smiled one of his beaming, gap-toothed expressions of pleasure. "Of course. Together we will paint and look at things. And maybe go hungry. But maybe not, who can tell? For now, let's find supper."

Arthur surveyed the little town, noting that the camp of the 13th cavalry was south of the El Paso and Western tracks and next to a well-traveled road leading out of Mexico. Most of the homes and businesses lay to the northeast where another, smaller road led off into the desert. An air of impermanence hung over the place, as if at any moment the flimsy houses and crooked buildings could disappear, blow away in the wind, leaving the land the way it had been — empty, shimmering with waves of heat and sun-light.

He didn't like what he was feeling, an uneasiness that caused him to note the location of buildings and highways, escape routes and safe houses. He didn't like it, but on the other hand he'd come in search of a fight, and, if his instinct was right, he was about to find one.

"Let's get back before dark," he said. "I want to interview this Seese fellow."

George Seese, a journalist for the Associated Press, greeted Arthur and Lucas with a firm handshake. "Glad to meet another writer," he said. "Sit down, and I'll tell you what I know, which isn't much. Everybody lies, or at least they don't let on what they know. What've you heard?"

"That Villa contacted you."

"He did. Sent me a message saying he wanted amnesty, but, since then, nothing. I've been sitting here, waiting and wondering. Did he mean it, or was it just another of his tricks?"

Arthur couldn't stay still but prowled the room, glancing out the window into the dark. Not a light burned anywhere, and the street was deserted. "Why would he pick Columbus?" he asked. "There's more important border towns."

Seese lit a cigar and sat back in his chair. "I know it looks like a bunch of shacks, but there's a lot a money in that bank, and, if Villa could take the Army camp, he'd have his hands on rifles, horses, supplies, all the things he doesn't have now. So all we can do is wait and see."

"I don't like it."

Seese drew on his cigar until the tip glowed. "Who does? Sleep with one eye open, and hope when he comes, if he comes, he doesn't come shooting."

The moon had set making darkness complete.

Three miles west of Columbus, Villa's army crossed the border and rode steadily east, the sound of hoofs muffled by deep sand, the jingling of bits and spurs unnoticed in the great and mysterious distance of the desert.

At the drainage ditch beside the north/south highway, the army divided, one group continuing east, the other south to Camp Furlong where, with shouts of *"¡Viva Méjico!"* both opened fire — on stables and barracks and on the houses where some of the officers and their families were quartered. At first the night shrouded them and added to the confusion, and then someone set fire to the hotel.

At the first sound of gunfire, the three Americans woke and jumped to their feet. On Arthur's advice, they'd slept in their clothes, ready for action, but cautious looks out the window showed nothing except unidentifiable gunfire.

"Jesus!" Arthur shouted. "I can't tell who's shooting who!"

Lubitsch pulled him back. "Keep your head down. You won't see if you're dead." Then he raised his head and sniffed the air like a massive hound.

Cautiously he opened the door and peered down the hall. "The hotel is burning," he announced. "Out the window we go. From the pan into the fire as somebody said."

"They're burning us out?" Of them all, Lucas was the most stunned. In his whole life he'd never pictured himself in the midst of a battle he couldn't see, hunted and helpless.

"Come, come!" Lubitsch opened the window and pulled himself through, then reached back for Lucas. "Hurry!"

Lucas scrambled out with Arthur close behind, and they crouched in a row beside the wall in what became a vain attempt to hide.

"Damn' fools," Arthur said. "They've lit up the whole town. Now those machine guns we heard can go to work."

"And now we go out where it's dark," Lubitsch said. "Now we hide and watch and wait, and you'll have your story."

Seese's window flew open, and he crawled out beside them. "Clever little bastard," he said. "I guess now we can tell what his plan was. Fake us out. But it sounds like our boys know what they're doing."

"And what I'm doing is getting away from this building before it falls." Lubitsch got to his feet. "You can talk or you can come."

Somewhere a baby was crying, its terrified wail piercing the roar of flames, the thunder of gunfire, the screams of people trapped in their homes by armed soldiers.

"Go on," Lucas urged. "I'll find you."

Lubitsch guessed his intention. "Be careful. If you find it, and it keeps yelling, *they* will find you and kill you."

"I'm not afraid of that any more." The words came out, and he recognized them. Death was all around, visible and invisible, but somewhere a child was screaming for its life.

His friends darted into the shadows, and he made his way toward a small house that appeared abandoned except for the child. At the sound of booted feet, he ducked behind a water trough, his breath coming hard. Smoke from the fire burned in his lungs, and desperately he stifled a fit of coughing as two armed *Villistas* passed by. Cautiously, then, he crept to the door that sagged open. What had happened to the parents? Would he find them dead? Bullets thudded into the adobe wall beside his head, and he threw himself inside onto the dirt floor and lay still, struggling for breath.

The baby lay on a cot on one corner, its cries subsiding into sobs, a prelude to sleep despite the battle outside. He thought it was a girl, tiny, with dark eyes and a thatch of dark hair, and, as she looked up at him, her mouth opened in what seemed to be surprise.

"Don't cry again, for God's sake," he whispered as he bent down to pick her up, realizing that he'd never picked up a baby before and had no idea what to do after he did, except to escape somehow onto the desert away from the fighting. He was amazed to find her warm and sturdy, and even more amazed when she turned and nuzzled him, seeking a breast. He laughed, then caught himself. Nothing to laugh at in this situation, and no telling what would happen once he went back outside. He could hear sporadic bursts of fire from American machine guns, and the fire at the hotel had spread so that it seemed half the town was burning.

Cautiously he stepped out into the street and around the back of the house. Beyond was safety in the shadows of mesquites, the dips and hollows where small washes criss-crossed the desert.

Clutching the baby in both arms, he began to run, stumbling over stones, and then tripping and falling, twisting himself so as not to crush the child. As he got to his feet, he saw the black horse, its rider staring down at him.

Now it would happen. Now he would die, here in this town that squatted like a mirage on the border, a place he'd never heard of, involved in a war that had no name. Fear made him reckless.

"Aren't you going to shoot?"

"I don't make war on little children, *Señor Artista*." The voice was rough with what sounded, incredulously, like laughter.

"You!" In the pale gray light that signaled the approach of dawn, he saw once again the face he'd never forgotten, fleshy, cruel, clever, but not without humor, as if he was toying with his victim.

"Where is your friend who writes?"

Lucas shifted the baby in his arms. "I'll find him. When this is over."

"It won't be over for a long while. And perhaps you won't find him. It's like I said, perhaps. No one can be trusted, not even your friends."

"I can't believe that," Lucas said, with a stubbornness he hadn't known he possessed.

"As you wish." Even in the dark, the shrug of the shoulders, the gleam of the bandoleers were obvious. "Now take the baby and go before I change my mind. And when you draw me again, draw me here, in your country. On land that belonged to the poor who have no voice."

Gravely Lucas nodded. He had been issued an order, and like a good soldier he would follow it. "Yes, sir. I will."

"Good. Now go!" Villa wheeled his horse and rode south at a full gallop.

In the aftermath of the raid, Lucas didn't have a chance to talk about what had happened, and later he found he wanted to keep the meeting to himself, a drama that was only his, a minor event in the midst of a larger, historic one.

Fortunately the reunion of an hysterical mother with her daughter had prevented anyone from asking him questions he didn't want to answer. Over and over, she kissed his hands, making him a hero, so that he blushed and stammered, and wished she would leave him to visualize the painting he would make — mountains, desert, yellow poppies, and the fierce little man on horseback, staring out with dogged but fiery determination.

Later, he, Lubitsch, Arthur, and George Seese wandered around the damaged town with its smoking ruins and bullet-riddled walls, and watched the cavalry troop in disciplined formation take off in pursuit of the *Villistas*.

"They won't catch him," Lucas said.

"How do you know?"

"Because it's not his time. He has something he has to do."

"And you have discovered what it is?" Lubitsch asked.

"No. I just know he's not going to give up. It's not in him to quit. He loves his people, and he loves what he's doing."

"And I'll love it when we take the wagon and go on. Somewhere. Anywhere, like nomads, Bedouins, those Mongol people with the felt tents, or Coronado in search of gold."

His picturesque description made Lucas laugh, although it added to his growing excitement. Every day history was being made — his own and the world's, and he was alive to witness it, capture it on canvas if he could.

In those great valleys, in the mountains and cañons and deserts, others had come before — Aztecs, Mayans, the people of the Mimbres, Apaches, Spaniards, men and women of all nations, young and old, sick and well, but every one hopeful — of riches perhaps, or perhaps only for a secure place of their own, the challenge of a new country.

His fingers itched with the need to begin. Still laughing he said: "Let's hurry. There's so much to do."

A Pair to Draw To

It was on the boat coming back from Buenos Aires that Janine and I disappeared. In place of Janine Longstreet and Stella Purdy, on the lam from the law and the men we'd run with to Paraguay, we became Stella White and Janine Black.

Janine and I had figured, when we left New Mexico in a hurry with Harvey and Hull and half the Pinkerton Agency's detectives on our trail, that we'd find a ranch in Paraguay, have lots of servants, and be able to buy ourselves pretty clothes. That all happened, but there were a lot of women in pretty clothes around, and Hull and Harvey pretty soon figured on getting to know them, instead of us — their wives who'd lived in a shack and watched over the money they stole for more years than I care to tell. For that, and being faithful, and keeping our mouths shut, they owed us.

Whatever, there we were, Janine and me with nothing to do but change our clothes four times a day, play cards — and we got good at that — boss the servants in a language nobody could really understand, and, once in a while, ride out and look over the place all that money had bought. And maybe call on the neighbors, except the closest was twenty miles away, and we didn't

183

speak their language, either, so what was the use?

Meantime, Harvey and Hull got up to their old tricks, gambling and rustling cattle. That was OK, but making eyes at the twin daughters of Don Diego Valenzuela was something else.

One night, Janine and I sat down at the big table in the big dining room all by ourselves and were served our dinner. I didn't have any appetite. I was too busy thinking about Hull making a fool of himself over one or the other of those twins who I never did learn to tell apart, and I bet he and Harvey never did, either. Across the table, Janine picked at her own food, no hungrier than I was.

I tossed down my fork. "You happy here?" I asked.

She looked at me out of those green eyes of hers. "Hell," she said, "I was happier back in New Mexico, living in that shack with something to do besides look at myself in a mirror."

"Me, too."

"It sounded good though, didn't it? I mean, all of us coming here. Starting over, and no damned law on our tail. It *was* good for a while." She pushed the meat around in the rice on her plate.

"You still in love with Harvey?"

She snorted. Loud. Janine never holds back. "Back then I was. At least I thought so. But down here . . . now. . . ." She snorted again. "He's turned into a real tinhorn. He's not the Harvey I knew."

I knew what she meant. Those two men had changed so much it's a wonder we didn't holler "rape" when they got around to getting into our beds. I'd been thinking about home — the high desert country — mountains, sand, mesquite, greasewood, and how it smells after a rain, so sweet you could bottle it. Paraguay, on the other hand, was rivers and marsh, grass, funny-looking trees, and air so heavy you could hang your hat on it.

"I want to go home," I said.

"Sure. You remember we're wanted back there, too, just like them. I bet they've got our pictures all over, and I'll be damned if I'll go to jail on their account."

"Nobody has our picture," I reminded her. "Nobody ever even saw us except that once in El Paso, and they didn't know who we were. Anyhow, nobody cares about us. We weren't the ones sticking up all those banks and trains."

Her eyes turned to slits, and I knew she was thinking about money. Janine always thinks about money, one reason we got along so well. She said: "We ought to clean them out and run."

"We could. They wouldn't miss us for a week."

She snorted again. "That's what I meant."

Janine and I go back a long ways, since childhood. It was just our luck that we'd fallen in love with two of the worst outlaws New Mexico had ever seen, worse even than Butch Cassidy and Blackjack Ketchum. But luck can be changed.

I lifted my glass of wine. It caught the candlelight and shone like a star. "Here's to us."

We drank. Knocked back a glass and poured another, and another after that, giggling like kids, except we weren't kids. We were two women who were ignored, bored, and about to take our lives into our own hands.

In the end it was easy. We waited till Harvey and Hull went off on another rustling or smuggling or flirtation trip — they never told us, and we never asked — then we packed our bags, one each for clothes and jewelry, another for enough money to keep us a while. A good thing our husbands didn't believe in banks. Of course, they wouldn't, knowing how easy it was to rob one. They'd carted in a big safe that sat in what they called their "office" and, unfortunately for them, had given us the combination.

"This is kind of like stealing from ourselves," I said to Janine.

She stuffed another wad of bills into her sack. "Look at it as back pay for all those years we hid the take under the floor and waited, scared to death they'd end up on a plank at some photographer's."

"At least we could've stayed home," I muttered, hoisting my sack over my shoulder and being astonished that so much money could weigh so little.

We left on horseback. Ignacio went with us. Down there, no lady goes any place by herself, probably because jealous husbands think they have to guard their little treasures. It's a system that doesn't work, but nobody wants to admit that, least of all the husbands.

That was in 1924. From the newspapers we got that were usually a couple months old, we knew that back in the States ladies had got the vote, were cutting their hair, showing their legs, and throwing their corsets away. And about time, too. But in South America we might as well have been living in a convent.

"Freedom, here we come." I waved good bye to the big, stone *hacienda* we'd lived in like prisoners. Not Harvey's and Hull's fault really. They just didn't know how it was going to be down there, and like a couple of kids let out of school they ran wild.

Janine kicked her horse into a lope. "Let's just get the hell out!"

It took four days to get to the coast. We had to skirt around marshes and cut through a patch of jungle that pressed down on our heads like a dark blanket. In the city it took another two days finding passage out, and all the time I kept looking over my shoulder, expecting to be kidnapped and taken back to the ranch. I drove Janine crazy.

"Quit doing that!" she snapped. "You're making me nervous. And, besides, if you think it, it'll happen, and then what?"

"I'll scream."

She gave me a look. "Yeah. And ten men

would come running to help grab the wicked wives."

"It's not us," I said. "It's the money they'd be after."

"Isn't it always?"

Finally, though, we boarded the ship, stowed our sacks in the closet in our cabin, and went up on deck to watch South America disappear.

"Good riddance," Janine said.

"What'll we do when we get home?" I wondered. "I mean with the rest of our lives?"

She shrugged. "Something'll turn up."

What turned up was Schuyler Mayhew — short, round, bald-headed, and filthy rich.

"Good day, ladies," he said, lifting his straw hat and showing his cue-ball head. "Lovely day, isn't it?"

Janine let him have it with her green eyes. "Lovely," she said.

"Permit me to introduce myself. I'm Schuyler Mayhew. Of the Philadelphia Mayhews," he added as if that meant something.

I wanted to laugh, but Janine stepped on my toe.

"I'm Janine Black, and this is Stella . . ."

"White," I put in, for no reason I could think of except association.

Schuyler raised his eyebrows to where his hair should have been. "If I might ask, what are two ladies like yourselves doing down here alone?"

Janine was slick-tongued, a talent she'd been born with and had honed with Harvey who

188

could talk his way out of anything, or any jail, come to think of it. "We inherited a ranch. One we didn't need, so we came to sell it and now are on our way home."

"A ranch, eh?"

"Cattle," she said. "Thousands of acres, but not anything we wanted to bother with."

Schuyler was impressed. I could tell by the new respect I saw in his eyes. "I hope you weren't cheated," he said. "Down here, one never knows."

Janine arched an eyebrow and put on her great lady act that she'd perfected over the years. "I never discuss money. Now, if you'll excuse us?"

"Of course, of course. I hope I didn't offend. I was merely making conversation." He took off his hat again.

"No offense, Mister Mayhew," she said.

"Then perhaps I might have the pleasure of taking you ladies to dinner."

"That would be nice." She took my arm and pulled me away.

Inside our cabin, I let out the laugh I'd been holding in. "What goes through your head?" I wanted to know. "Why different names?"

"Look, we can't go back as who we are. They're not sure what we look like, but they might know our names. The Pinkertons or some law man some place would catch us in a week. And we're not poor, so we might as well say so. That old man wouldn't even look at us if he thought we were broke."

"Who cares about him?"

"He's rich, he's got connections."

"To who? Are you planning on being some old man's fancy woman?"

"Fancy, schmancy," she said. "I figured it out all those years when there wasn't anything to do *but* sit and figure. It's who you know that counts, not who you are."

"And now we're not even us." I felt lost all of a sudden.

She whipped around. "Oh, hell, of course, we're us. But we've got to think about the future. That dough isn't going to last forever. And then what? Then who'll we be? Two old ladies on charity, is what. Well, let me tell you, I grew up poor, but I don't aim to be poor ever again. What you do is your problem."

The trouble was, I hadn't thought about the future. I'd been too busy living in the present. "I just figured we'd buy a house and live in it," I said. "Some place back where we belong. What's wrong with that?"

"Depends on the house."

"Just a house. Big enough to take in boarders if it comes to it."

She sniffed. "You mean like old maids and broken-down cowboys? No thanks. But investing in real estate's a good idea."

The way her mind was going was beyond me. "Where'd you learn about investing? Where'd you learn to think like that?"

"While you were back there changing clothes all day and doing card tricks, I was reading the papers." She sat down on the bed cross-legged, like an Indian. "I read them cover to cover, especially the finance pages, and they started me thinking. You use money to make more money is the way I see it."

There was sense in that. Like I said, Janine has always been good about money, and what she said started *me* thinking. After a minute, I said: "We could buy a hotel."

"A retreat," she corrected.

"For rich old men like Schuyler out there." Before the words were out of my mouth, I knew I'd struck gold.

She grinned ear to ear. "That's it, kid. That's it. A gentleman's retreat. And they'll pay. And keep paying."

"We'll get famous."

"I don't want to get famous," she said. "But you can bet your ass I want to get rich."

We had been at sea three days and were sitting on deck with Mayhew hovering around us as if he were handcuffed, when he suddenly began to cough and couldn't stop. I thought he'd swallowed something. We had been drinking coffee and eating little cakes, and I stood up, ready to whack him between his shoulders, but he waved me off, then mopped his face with his handkerchief.

"Are you all right?" I asked.

"Yes, yes. Just a nasty cough." He sounded scared.

"You ought to take something for it," Janine said.

"I am, my dear. I'm taking a sea voyage. Doctor's orders. Fresh air and rest and all that."

"But that won't help," I told him. "You want dry air, not all this damp."

"What she means," Janine said, picking up my cue, "is that you really ought to go to the Southwest. You'd be cured in no time. We've had several guests come to us just for that reason."

He perked right up, and I felt my heart drop into my shoes for fear he'd insist on coming with us to nowhere. But Janine was quick.

"While we've been gone, we were having some work done on the house, but who knows what's gotten finished. Probably nothing. You know how that is, I'm sure."

"I do." He shook his head at the thought of workmen taking advantage. "You need someone to look after your affairs, my dear. Workmen will get away with whatever they can, you know, especially with a lady."

Lord! I thought. *Next thing, he'll propose!* I sat up and did my best to change the subject by talking about the country as I remembered it, and only succeeded in making myself miserable. Schuyler got so interested that he asked a hundred questions which we answered as best we could. Most of them dealt with whether or not we accepted payment from our guests. We did.

And whether having guests was an inconvenience. As angels of mercy, we assured him that we were only too happy to bring health back to our good friends. He was easy to convince because he seemed to want to believe in the whole proposition.

I had some doubts. "Is what we're doing illegal?" I asked Janine later.

"Don't be silly. We're only trying to make a living."

"Yes, but we sounded like a pair of cons. We sounded like Harvey talking a blue streak."

She was filing her nails and buffing them with a piece of cotton. "What did you think? That we were going to be queens of England?"

"I don't think I thought," I said, sounding foolish.

"Better start then. Or let me do the talking, if it makes you nervous."

It did, but she'd been right about one thing. Neither of us would ever end up queen of England.

That night we sailed into rough weather, and the next day we stayed in our cabin, taking turns being sick.

"Never again," I gasped after a bout with the washbasin. "I never want to see the ocean as long as I live."

"Me, neither."

"Mayhew wants to marry you." I was getting good at changing the subject.

She gagged. "Please. Bigamy isn't exactly my

line. Yours, either. And, besides, he's got breath like a grizzly. So I'll say I'm a widow with no intentions of ever risking my heart again." Sitting there, pale-faced, one hand at her throat, she turned into the grieving widow in front of my eyes.

"You should've gone on the stage."

She laughed. "We are on the stage, in case you haven't noticed. And you don't do too bad yourself."

"As Stella White."

"Exactly. And when we get off this stinking ship, we're headed home quick as we can to find ourselves that little retreat for ailing gentlemen. Mayhew's on the hook, and we don't have any time to lose."

We sailed into New York Harbor, and, at the sight of the Statue of Liberty rising up out of the sea, I broke down and cried. It seemed she was welcoming me home after ten years, regardless of who I was or wasn't, welcoming everybody, rich and poor, man or woman, and I thought I'd been a damned fool to turn my back on her just because I'd married an outlaw.

Janine stood beside me, dabbing her own eyes, which surprised me. She wasn't sentimental, and she was tougher than I was, but she felt it, too — the power, the promise. Even Schuyler was struck, and kept nodding his bald head. He'd taken off his hat in a show of respect. "A great lady. Very great, indeed."

In spite of our plan to get West fast, we stayed in New York for a week, seduced by the sights, the shops, and our need for decent clothes. It was like being in a big beehive, buzzing day and night, and after ten years of quiet we both loved it.

Schuyler took us to the opera, which didn't impress me as much as the people in the audience — all those women in fancy gowns and jewels on the arms of sleek-looking men — and to Wall Street, which impressed Janine to the point where I thought she was going to drool.

"What power!" she kept saying. "All that dough!"

"Gambling's what it is. I'd rather play poker," I said.

Schuyler saw his chance to show off. Then and there he gave us a long lecture on finance, and for once I listened and was impressed in spite of myself.

That night, after dinner, he handed each of us a small, beautifully wrapped box. "Mementos of a lovely voyage with two lovely ladies," he said.

Inside Janine's box was a diamond bracelet. In mine I found a diamond brooch in the shape of a butterfly.

"I can't accept this. It's too much," Janine said, although her fingers held onto the thing so hard it would have taken a crowbar to pry them off.

"Of course, you can," he said. "You made my trip a pleasant one. Both of you. And I look forward to seeing you again as soon as I'm invited."

He looked at me, and his eyes twinkled. "And to a hand or two of poker with Missus White."

At that point I started to like him. He was a gentleman, and, God knew, I'd seen enough of the other kind to tell the difference. I leaned across the table and patted his arm. "I cheat," I said.

He twinkled harder. "So do we all, my dear. The crowning achievement is not being caught at it."

It was impossible not to twinkle back. "What a clever way to put it."

"When you're as old as I am," he said, "you'll find there are hundreds of ways to say the same thing. It makes for interesting conversation, not to mention literature."

I thought that playing cards with a shrewd old hand like him might be sort of like playing with loaded pistols, so I just smiled and nodded and kept my mouth shut.

The next morning we took the train West.

Mostly I looked out the window at the country we went through, looked and looked till my eyes got dried out, and still I couldn't stop.

Hurry, hurry, hurry. The words echoed in my head in time with the clacking wheels. Up ahead was home where I belonged and never should have left.

Suddenly there were the High Plains, as empty, as windblown as ever, and the sky wrapped around them that pure, pale blue I thought I'd never see again, and cattle grazing, brown specks on green earth. And then we were among mesas, and beyond them were mountains with snow still on their tops.

Briefly I wondered if Hull was missing this country that he knew even better than I did; if maybe he wasn't even missing me and wishing he'd led another kind of life, settled down and stayed put. But he wasn't made right for that, not Hull, who, if you told him no, went out and did the opposite just to prove he could. It was the daring in him I'd fallen in love with, not the man himself. Not the man who'd promised me riches and jewels and then left me alone to amuse myself with them. I sighed.

Janine looked up. "What's that for?"

"I was thinking about Hull."

She gave her usual snort. "Forget him. He's got what he wants, and we're here." She giggled. "A good thing. If he stuck up this train, I'd have to swallow my bracelet."

I laughed at the notion. "You would, too."

"Of course. One thing I'll say for Schuyler. He's not cheap, and he knows how to have fun."

"I kind of like him." I pulled a deck of cards out of my pocket. "But I have a hunch I'd better practice up."

"Yeah," she said. "Just remember. We have one rule. The house wins. Always. And the house is us."

We got off the train at Portillo, a town with a

long history — as stagecoach stop, freighting dépôt, cattle town, and, briefly, when a vein of silver was discovered, rip-roaring mining camp. When the silver played out, some folks stayed, and new people drifted in — Easterners who liked the scenery, the climate, the hunting, and who demanded goods and service. Best of all, even though we knew the town, the town didn't know us. Our shack in the cañon had been fifty miles southwest over a bad trail. We'd got on the train for South America in Portillo, unnoticed, unremarked, but the place itself had stuck in our minds. We registered at the hotel, took a walk, ate a decent lunch, and then set off to look at property.

Lester Foulks, the real estate agent, was a nervous little man with a tic at the corner of his mouth. Watching, I discovered that it twitched whenever he told an outright lie or even shaded the truth, which was about every five minutes. Nervous habits betray people — every card player knows that — so I watched, listened, looked at houses, and said no to every one, though I had to discourage Janine from making an offer on what appeared to be the ideal place.

"There's something he's not telling," I whispered. "Trust me."

To Foulks I said: "There must be something else. Large. Private."

He twitched, then brightened. "There's the old Jarvis House. The price just got cut in half. It's up the mountain a little ways, though."

"Why is that? About the price?"

He looked away. "Been empty a while. Too big for most folks." He cleared his throat. "Truth to tell, it was a rest home for lungers right after the war. Some folks think that ain't healthy."

"Show us," I said, and got back in the car.

The road was in sorry shape. We'd gone a couple miles when a tire blew.

"We'll walk," I told him. "You change the tire and come get us."

So Janine and I were alone when we reached the big adobe house with its wide front porch and two wings on either side. Tiles were missing from the roof, and some windows were boarded up, but there was a lure to the place, like it was calling to me.

"This is it!" I said.

"It's a mess!"

"Not when we get through, it won't be. Let's walk around."

That's how we discovered the sun porch, once glassed-in and facing south, and the walled garden now filled with weeds, shattered tiles, and broken glass. A rattlesnake lay under a bush taking advantage of the shade.

"Probably crawling with the damn' things," Janine muttered. "And here we are without our pistols."

Cascabel. The Spanish word came to me. The word for bells and rattlesnakes. "Casa Cascabel," I said. "That's the name! It's perfect!"

"We haven't even been inside. God knows

what's in there. Probably bats. And fixing this won't be cheap."

"It takes money to make money, like you always say. Come on, let's look."

In the end, she gave in, charmed by the big living room with its two stone fireplaces, the eight bedrooms, and the idea that she could have an office of her own, complete with standing safe.

We bought it, fixed it, and by Thanksgiving were awaiting our first guests, Schuyler and a friend, Franklin Voorhees, who, we were told, was recovering from pneumonia.

I met their train, driving our new Ford, which Janine refused to touch after her first frantic attempt to stop it by calling — "Whoa!"

"We'll hire a driver," was her comment.

"For now, that's me."

"Think how it looks! Like we can't afford one!"

"But it's so much nicer to meet your friends yourself."

"My dear Missus White! How very nice of you to come for us!" Schuyler bent over my hand in his familiar gesture. "May I present Mister Voorhees."

Mister Voorhees looked like a good wind might blow him over. I hoped he wouldn't die on us and give us a bad name right off.

"Pleased to meet you," I said, and to Schuyler: "I hope you'll both enjoy your visit."

Voorhees nodded and smiled, and I decided he was either stupid or shy. Actually, I was wrong on both counts. The altitude had gotten to him, and he was asleep standing up.

Schuyler and I hustled him into the car, and we took off up the bumpy road, with Schuyler exclaiming over the scenery and asking me the name of every mountain and tree that he saw.

"It's just as you described it! Charming, charming!" he kept repeating until I pulled up at the gate to the house.

His reaction was all I'd hoped for. "Why . . . why . . . it's sumptuous! I admit, I thought you might have been fooling me, as people will try to do, you know, for one reason or another. But I see I was being cynical. You'll forgive me, I hope?"

I hopped out and gave him a smile. "Forget it. And welcome to Casa Cascabel."

Together we bustled Voorhees inside, where Janine met us full of concern. "Is he sick?"

"Exhausted, poor fellow. He had a bout with pneumonia, as I told you, and the trip was tiring."

"It's the altitude," I told her. "He's one of those that's not used to it."

"Bed," she said firmly. "The best place for him. I'll have Abelardo take him something to eat when he wakes up. Dinner's in an hour. And it's a pleasure to see you again."

Schuyler bowed. "The pleasure is mine."

To tell the truth, it was fun having those two

around. They stayed a month, and paid us well, and, when Voorhees, who we started calling Frank, got better, we all went on excursions in the car. To the Indian reservation first — neither one of them had ever seen a real Indian, and they exclaimed, posed for photos, and bought rugs, baskets, and pots like they were candy and had them crated and shipped home — then to a ghost town, a collection of falling-down shacks and tumbleweeds, and to one of the banks that Harvey and Hull had cleaned out to the last penny. The bank had a little exhibit in the lobby — phony photos of Harvey and Hull and framed newspaper accounts of the robbery, like it was something to be proud of — losing all that money, being out-foxed by those two.

"Interesting psychology," Schuyler said, when we'd left and were eating lunch.

"What is?"

"Those outlaws. Longstreet and Purdy. They got away with hundreds of thousands. One wonders why they kept at it so long."

Janine snorted, although she tuned down the noise for appearances.

I said: "Maybe they were just tired of being poor. That's understandable."

"But when does one have enough? It seems they went on for the fun of it, don't you think?"

· I hadn't really thought about why they went on stealing, long after they had more money than any ten people needed, but, looking back, I realized it had turned into a game with them, a challenge to see how much they could get away with, a defiance of the law men and detectives who were always two steps behind.

"I guess," I said slowly, "they wanted to see how far they could go. You're right. After a while, it wasn't the money, it was the fun of it. And when the law got too close, they high-tailed it out of here. There's no point being rich behind bars, is there?"

Janine kicked me under the table.

Frank had been listening to the exchange and frowning. He said: "Where do you think they went?"

Janine kicked me again, harder. I kicked her back with a vengeance, then shrugged. "Who knows? The world's a big place."

"It's shrinking," Frank said in his slow way. "One of these days we'll know what's happening everywhere within minutes."

"God help us!" Janine exclaimed, attempting to end the discussion. "I've got enough troubles of my own."

We all laughed. But I had the horrible thought that maybe we'd been harboring a pair of detectives and weren't as smart as we figured, proving that we had to be more careful about who we took in and what we said.

So when Frank asked me if I'd ever actually seen Longstreet or Purdy, being as we lived in the area, I swallowed hard before I answered.

"Maybe," I said. "Only I didn't know it. I mean, you pass people in the street, but you never think about who they are. At least I don't. And I don't make a habit of staring at strangers, either."

Schuyler chuckled. "Well put." And then to Frank: "This woman has actually admitted that she cheats at cards, but you'd never know it to look at her, would you?"

"Speaking of cards," Janine put in, "we should play a hand or two tonight if we're not exhausted by the time we get home."

"Excellent!" Schuyler was beaming. "I've been meaning to suggest it myself, but your company's been too delightful to waste on poker playing."

"Flatterer." She stood up. "If we want to get back before dark, we'd better go."

On the way out, she grabbed my arm. "Are you ready for this?"

"As I'll ever be," I said, thinking of the cards I'd so carefully marked and then resealed with the help of a hot iron and a lot of patience, and scared out of my wits that I'd do or say something without knowing it. I guessed it would be a long evening.

I was winning, and not because I was cheating, either. Maybe it was just luck, or maybe I was being suckered by a master into betting the farm on a pair of deuces.

A study of Schuyler didn't tell me anything. For once his face was bland, a real poker face. Even his eyes had no expression behind his spectacles. Damn him! I'd have bet he was throwing his good cards away, but since looking at the discards was out, I couldn't prove it unless somehow I could sneak a look. So I waited, and watched, and won some more.

When it was my deal, I swept up the cards that were on the table, with the discards on the bottom, and, under pretext of aligning the pack, took a quick look. Sure enough, I spotted an ace and a wild joker that only Schuyler could have thrown away. Well, two could play that game. I dealt, let Schuyler open, then Frank raise, then Janine. I folded and sat back.

Frank won the hand. On the next hand, I did the same, and the one after that, and Schuyler peered at me over the tops of his glasses. "Your luck seems to have changed."

"It was bound to, wasn't it?"

A flash of humor lit his eyes. "Of course."

Under cover of the table, I unfastened the catch of the bracelet I wore — smoky topaz from South America, a present from a husband who had taught me most of what I knew about poker, and who, in spite of everything, I still remembered with a feeling much like regret.

I sighed, and Schuyler noticed. "What's the matter, my dear?"

"Nothing."

"From the look on your face, it's more than that. Surely not simply a run of bad luck?"

"No," I said, choosing my words carefully. "I was thinking about my dear, dead husband, and how he loved a good poker game."

On my right, Janine turned stiff as a stick.

"Ah." Schuyler leaned toward me. "I'm sorry. You never talk about him. What was his name?"

Good God! What *was* his name anyhow? Speechless, I stared at him.

Janine saved me. "It hurts her to talk about it," she whispered.

He accepted her explanation with a shamed expression. "Forgive me. We won't mention it again. It's your deal, Stella."

I lifted my hand to wipe my fake tears, and the bracelet flew off onto the floor. That little diversion gave me the chance to deal as I wanted — not to myself, but to Janine. After all, as she'd reminded me, *the house was us*.

She had two queens showing.

"A pair to draw to. Much like yourselves," Schuyler said, pondering his hole cards. He stayed in.

Janine was pleased. "You golden-tongued devil." She pushed all her chips into the pot.

I folded.

Schuyler called.

"Four queens," she said with an air of triumph. She even had a pair of aces and a joker she didn't need.

He looked at me. "Have you been cheating, Stella?"

"Have you?"

"I'll never tell. We all must keep some secrets."

At that, I stood up. "Speaking of secrets, shall

we have some of Abelardo's whisky before we go up to bed?"

"Yes," Frank said. He'd developed a real taste for the stuff Abelardo turned out in his still up the mountain. Those were Prohibition years, and everybody we knew had a still somewhere, or, if they didn't, it was easy enough to go down to Mexico and bring it back or wait for the weekly smuggler's mule train to arrive at some agreed-upon but well-hidden spot. Once the barrels were unloaded, the mules were turned loose, and they headed for home and a good meal and another trip. Looking back, it's obvious that Janine and I weren't the only ones cheating. The whole world was conspiring to cheat the government, and doing pretty well at it.

Frank raised his glass. "When I get home, I'm recommending you to all my friends. *Skoal!*"

"*Salud, dinero, y amor,*" I corrected. "That's what we say out here."

"Translate, please."

"Health, money, and love . . . *and the time to enjoy them*. That's the motto of this place."

Frank hiccupped. "Like I said, I'm telling everybody."

He was as good as his word, and so was Schuyler. For the next years, we had a stream of health-seeking, hard-drinking visitors, all of them men with money to pay. Our bankroll kept growing.

"The old fools," Janine called them, behind

their backs, of course.

We counted our money and invested prudently in stocks and real estate. Our old gentlemen were a mine of financial information, which we used to advantage. Soon we were a ranch, running cattle and keeping a few horses for guests to ride. It was splendid!

And then came 1929 and the years right after. For the first time we had empty rooms and months with nothing to do but talk to each other to break the silence.

"This can't go on," Janine declared. "Or can it?"

We were sitting at dinner, the two of us, and I had the feeling we had come 'round in a circle, ending where we'd started — except a good deal richer.

"At least, we've got money," I said. "And this place. That's more than a lot of people have." There were men we knew who'd jumped out of windows or blown off their heads after the market crashed, and the road into town was filled with farmers headed out of the Dust Bowl, their cars and trucks piled high with what looked like junk to me but was obviously necessary to them. And worse, they all looked hungry. "At least, we won't starve," I added.

"And I'm bored. This place is a pain." She fiddled with her glass. "The worst part is, there's nobody left with enough money to buy it."

"We can't sell!" Her attitude had startled me. Looking around, I realized I loved every inch of the Casa Cascabel — its beamed ceilings and tile floors, its porches and patios, the little garden that I'd planted with Abelardo's help, the chickens, cows, horses, even the barn cats, owl-eyed and wild. "It's home," I said, and heard my voice wobble.

"Don't tell me you've turned house *Frau*."

The mockery in her tone got under my skin. "So what if I have?"

"Oh, hell," she said. "I'm getting bitchy in middle age. Forget it. I know you love it here. It's just me. I can't seem to settle down. All this peace and quiet's driving me crazy." She drummed her fingers on the table and looked at them, admiring the rings she wore. "Maybe I'm just a party girl long in the tooth and hating every minute of it."

We weren't getting any younger, and that was the cold, hard fact. Janine had been dying her red hair for a couple years, and I was about to start, although why I should bother with nobody to see me was a question I'd asked myself just that morning.

"So what do you want to do?" I asked.

"Get out of here. Travel. Be in a city where's there's some action."

"So go," I said. "I'll stay here and keep the place going. This damn' Depression can't last forever."

"By the time it's over, I might be in a wheelchair. And what'll you do here all by yourself?"

"Keep the garden. Ride the horses. Maybe

write my memoirs."

She snorted. "You? Write? Be serious. How do you know you can?"

I didn't, but I had a hankering to put down what was in my head, mainly for myself. Like tidying up a closet or a drawer and putting everything in order.

Before I could explain, Abelardo came in. "*Señoras,* there are two men outside who wish to speak with you."

"Now? Who are they?" Janine was annoyed.

"They didn't say, *señora.* Shall I tell them to come back tomorrow?"

She got up. "No. I'll go see." Her face brightened. "Maybe they're new customers. God knows that would be a relief."

Her high heels clicked on the tile floor. I remember that — and the scream she let out a minute later.

Abelardo and I rushed out, frightened. She was standing in the middle of the living room, white-faced and staring at two men I didn't recognize. They were well-dressed, and one of them leaned heavily on an ornate walking stick.

Abelardo advanced on them, his hands made into fists, and I went to Janine. "What's happening?"

"A hell of a greeting," the one with the cane said.

Then I knew. It was *them.*

"What are you doing here? Are you nuts? What happened to your leg?" I went over to Hull and looked up into his face. He'd shaved his mustache, and his hair had gone gray, but his eyes were the same, black and unreadable.

"What? No kiss for your old man?" he said.

I took hold of myself before I started screeching, too. "My old man's dead."

" 'Fraid not." He looked like he knew a joke he wasn't telling.

Janine said: "I think we'd better sit down. It's going to be a long night."

It was, too. Everybody had some explaining to do, and at first we all talked at once and made no sense, and we weren't helped by drinking Abelardo's whisky that he was still making even though Prohibition was over.

It seemed that South America — at least the part we knew — was having a bloody war over which country owned what, and Harvey and Hull had got caught in the crossfire, not to mention the fact that they had been rustling beeves and had got away by the skin of their teeth, Hull with a bullet in his leg.

"I suppose you had to leave your money," Janine said, mean as a snake.

Harvey laughed. "Nope! It's safe in the bank. Thanks to you two. After you gals left, we decided it wasn't safe keeping the loot in the house, so don't worry. We didn't come to sponge off you."

"Then why did you?"

They looked foolish for a minute before Hull spoke up. "We got homesick."

"Bull!" Janine said.

"It's the truth. Besides, nobody knows us any more."

"Don't bet on it." She got up and went to the door and locked it. "You're not staying here. We can't afford to keep criminals. We've built up a decent business and can't take chances."

"Yeah, we heard all about it." Harvey was laughing. "How these two nice ladies, Janine Black and Stella White had a rest home up the mountain. And I said . . . 'Stella and Janine, huh? Is there two sets of them?' Well, looks like you've done all right for yourselves. Bilking old men and doing it legit. Pretty smart, I'd say, wouldn't you, Hull?"

Hull nodded. "But we figured you'd be in Denver or Frisco."

"We were homesick, too," I admitted. "At least I was. And we just kind of fell into the business. It's been fine. Until lately."

Hull was frowning. When he spoke, he sounded like a preacher at a funeral, sad and somber. "The whole damn' country is blowing away, Stel. We saw it, Harvey and me, from the train. In the cities, there's folks in line waiting for a hand-out. Hell, there's not anybody worth stealing from any more! Even the banks are broke. We were fixing to go to California, maybe open a saloon with a little gambling on the side, but I don't know. Seems like there's not enough money around to fill a saloon."

"Sure there is." Janine had been pacing around

like a lion in a cage, but she stopped suddenly, her eyes hard as stones. "Sure there is. Times like these, people drown their troubles in booze. Count me in. I was getting damn' hard up for fun out here in the country. If you'll have me, that is."

My mouth hung open, I was so flabbergasted. She looked at me, and laughed. "I know, I know, you want to stay here. That's up to you. As for me, I'll take my chances in the city. That's if you want my company, fellas."

"Only if you stay put," Harvey said. "No running off with the dough this time. That's a bad habit."

"Look who's talking."

"I got a right. Not every man would take back a woman who did what you did, you know."

She finished her drink and poured another, and tossed that one off, too. "And not every woman would be crazy enough to take back a man who left her sitting around the house wasting time," she said. "So we're even."

I remembered how we'd gotten drunk that last night in Paraguay, and how she'd looked, reckless, up for anything. I'd been the same. Then. But now was different. I'd become somebody else and was comfortable with it.

"Stel?" Hull fixed those black eyes on me. "How about it? I'm ready to forgive and forget."

It was that last that decided me. Forgive and forget, my foot! He wasn't the one who'd been cheated on, left to twiddle his thumbs in a place

213

where everything was different, even the language. And now it was all my fault. Never mind that, over the years I'd thought about him with a bit of regret for the times we'd had fun, the nights when I'd been sure I loved him, and he felt the same. But, like I said, I was another Stella. I ran a business, mostly on the up and up, or at least I gave back as good as I got. All those men who'd come out sick and left a damned sight better had got what they paid for. And, besides, there was the land — mountains, cañons, the valley where our cattle grazed, the yucca blooming in the spring, and the yellow daisies and asters in the fall, and how the air smelled sweet all the time with grass, or rain, or flowers I couldn't name but recognized just the same. What city — what man — could compare to that?

I stood up. "I'm not guilty of much of anything. Maybe we both have things to forget, but I forgot a long time ago. You don't want me like I am now, and I don't want you. No offense," I added, because I saw the muscles in his jaw get tight, and Hull could get nasty, as I knew very well. "I'm staying. This here's where I belong, and I probably shouldn't have left. You three go. I'll be here if you need a bolt-hole or just some place quiet. I'm glad you're both safe, and I hope you stay that way. We'll keep in touch, and I'll send Janine her share of the profits, if there are any. Is that all right?"

She opened her arms and gave me a big hug.

"Oh, damn, I'll miss you! It's been good, hasn't it?"

"It has." I figured she was on the verge of a crying jag, and patted her shoulder. "Don't worry about anything. Just go and have yourself a good fling. The door's always open."

A week later they boarded the train for California. Abelardo and I stood on the platform and waved till it disappeared.

"What now, *señora?*" His face was sad.

"Now we get ourselves a couple hands and go brand my calves. Then we'll worry. At least, we've got enough to eat, not like lots of folks."

After that I had a few guests, but it wasn't the same. Nothing was, and those two gents complained about everything — the food, the service, even the weather. It was summer, and it rained every afternoon, which pleased me but made them irritable.

I was glad to see the last of them, and did what I said I'd do. Start my memoirs. Every night I sat in front of the fire and scribbled away until Abelardo — and his wife, Rosaura, who did the cooking — thought I had lost my mind. Actually, I was enjoying myself — all those memories, good and bad, and all the people I'd known. I wasn't even surprised when the phone rang one night and I heard Schuyler on the other end.

"Long time no see," I said.

He hemmed. "Yes. Too long. I'd like to come out, if you have room."

That was a laugh. "Sure," I said. "When?"

"I can leave in a few days. I have something important I want to talk to you about."

"You're getting married!"

A dry chuckle followed that. "No, my dear. I'll tell you when I arrive."

When he got off the train, he looked old to me, although I'd thought he was old the first time we'd met.

"Are you all right?" I put my hand under his elbow in case he fell over.

"Let's go to the house," he said.

That's when I really started to worry, but I tucked him into the car and drove off.

"Still the same," he said, looking around with his usual enthusiasm. "It's good this place doesn't change. Comforting in a way."

That's how I felt, and told him so.

"I'll never forget your face when you first told me about your part of the country," he said. "You looked like you'd seen a vision. I was quite jealous, never having had that experience."

"Well, you have now." I pulled up in front of the door. "But there have been a few changes. Janine's gone. I hope you don't mind."

"Gone?" His eyebrows shot up. "Where to? For how long?"

"She got bored. Business hasn't been good, so she took off for California. The last I heard, she was on her way to Vancouver." The three of them, actually, but I thought I'd leave Harvey and Hull dead.

"Then it's just you."

"And Abelardo and Rosaura. And a cowboy."

"Ah." He nodded to himself like he was making a decision, but to me he said nothing, just went up the steps and into the house.

He'd brought a lot of luggage. I sent Abelardo out for it, then asked him which room he'd like, since they were all empty.

"Oh . . . the one with the little porch. The one facing the mountain. I've always loved to watch it at sunset. It makes me wish I could paint."

"Maybe you can." After all, if I could write down my story, what would it hurt if he played around with paint?

"Stella," he said, "you're remarkable."

"Me?"

"Yes. You with your complete faith in yourself and everyone else, too. It's a gift, my dear. Cherish it."

"If you say so." I was flustered. Praise from Schuyler came in rare doses and, sometimes, in a way I couldn't understand. "Why don't you go up? Dinner's the same time as always."

I watched him climb the stairs, which he did slowly, and again I wondered if something wasn't wrong.

Dinner was over, and we were sitting in front of the fire, Schuyler with his feet up on an ottoman, a brandy on the table beside him.

"A splendid meal, a fine fire, and your delightful company. What more could I ask?"

I smiled but didn't answer, hoping he'd get to the point.

He took a sip of brandy, then cleared his throat. "Now . . . I mentioned a proposition to you, and there's no point beating around the bush. The doctor's given me a year, more or less. No . . . don't interrupt." He waved a hand at me. "Just listen. I've lived a good life. No regrets but one. I've never married and have no children, at least not that I know of. No one to leave my estate to. Oh, I've got nieces and nephews, but they're a spoiled lot. Got too much as it is. And I've given all I'm going to charity. Let them make it on their own, I say. So what I thought is simply this. If you'll agree, that is. I'd like to stay here till the end, and you needn't worry I'll be a bother because I won't. And when it happens, I'd like to be buried here. What money I have, I'll leave to you. Only to you, since Janine has deserted the ship, so to speak. And, besides, she's always been the greedy one. Well. What do you say?"

I sat there, looking at my hands in my lap and feeling bad. No words came. Not a one.

"Surprised you, didn't I?" Amazingly his eyes still had the old twinkle. "Well, you won't be the only one when the Mayhew clan hears about it. What do you say, Stella?"

"I'm sorry." I was, too.

"We all go sometime."

"I know, but. . . ."

"You're avoiding the answer," he said. "Yes or no."

The truth was, I was fond of him. In lots of ways we were alike, although that sounds funny, considering. Then there was the fact that I enjoyed his company, particularly with the place empty and likely to stay that way. The money came last. I had enough for myself, but then, you never know. As clearly as if she was standing there, I heard Janine say — *For God's sake, say yes!*

"Yes," I repeated. "But not account of the money. You're welcome even if you don't have a cent."

"That's what I thought you'd say." He nodded at me, pleased. "You're a good woman, Stella. The best."

"Not really."

"Nonsense. You've done what you had to do like the rest of us."

"You don't know," I said. "You haven't any idea what I've done."

He chuckled. "Oh, I think I have."

"How?"

"Intuition. I thought you ladies were running a racket when I met you, and perhaps you were, but you were fun. And you made a success out of it. I admire success. It takes brains and hard work. So no matter what, I find you admirable. That's my privilege."

"You knew all the time?" It was hard to believe, but on the other hand Schuyler was shrewd.

"Let's just say I had a hunch, and I play my

hunches, much as you do. In any case, who you were and what you've done doesn't matter any more."

"But it does. I'm ashamed of myself," I said. "And you've always been so nice."

"Not always." He looked off into the fire. "You say that because that's the side of me you know best. But we're all many-faceted, a mix of good and bad, as I'm sure you know by now."

Put that way, what Janine and I had done didn't sound so bad, even if it was built on stolen money. "You make the most sense," I told him. "You should have been a priest or something."

His laugh was dry. "Never! It wouldn't have suited me at all. What's that in your chair?" He pointed at my tablet.

"Nothing."

"Something surely, or you wouldn't look so guilty."

Still the same Schuyler, never missing a move. "My memoir," I said. "And don't laugh."

"A good idea. And you'll show me when you're finished."

"Maybe." And maybe then he'd change his mind about me, not that it mattered. Except now, in a funny way, it did. It mattered a lot. "Promise you won't hate me?"

He made a steeple out of his fingers and propped his chin on them. For a minute the fire flashed on his spectacles so I couldn't see his eyes, but when I did, they were wise and kind. "I promise," he said. "Cross my heart."

So now I'm sitting here, and Schuyler is reading what I've written. I can't tell what he thinks; there's no expression on his face at all. It was a bad idea, showing him my life. He could turn me in, make me tell where Harvey and Hull are, even though I don't know for sure. I'm so dumb sometimes, not like Janine, who wouldn't have trusted her own grandmother with a quarter, let alone with her life. I've always looked for the best in people, and usually found it, unlike her, although even she was fond of old Schuyler.

He's put down my tablet, and he's looking at me, and he's laughing. Laughing, mind you! "What's funny?" For some reason, it makes me mad, him finding my life humorous.

"This!" He waves it at me. "You, Janine, me, this place. Even I couldn't have imagined all of it, and I've pulled some dandies in my day."

He has me confused, but he's still laughing, and, after a minute, I join in, because, come to think of it, it *is* funny. From a distance I can look at what I've written like it's about somebody else, and laugh at how wild we all were, and how young and foolish. Kind of like this country that, no matter what, was headed forward, taking risks but sure of its own strength.

"My, oh, my," Schuyler says, wiping his glasses that have gotten fogged up. "You make me wish I were young again. I'd have gone with you to Paraguay. And if I had, you'd never have left. We'd still be there living off the fat of the land and enjoying ourselves. Although, come to think of it, I like it better right here."

"Me, too. And I'm glad to just be me for a change. It's a relief. To tell the truth, I always felt a little bad about telling you all those lies."

He replaces his spectacles, and behind them his eyes are curious and sharp. He doesn't look like he's dying, and there's a part of me that wishes he wasn't.

He says: "It's a case of the end justifying the means if I ever heard of one. But never mind that. What will you do with your inheritance? It would please me to know."

I think that one over. Knowing him, there might be some string attached, but when I answer, it's honest because there's no point lying to him now.

"Why," I say, sounding like Janine, "I'll use it to make more money. After all, a girl has to earn a living somehow."

The Perseid Meteors

"We're having a meteor party and a celebration," Betsy said. "Roger finally got permission from the county to develop that hundred acres in the cañon. Come on over tomorrow night."

Personally I didn't think building more houses on an already over-crowded desert was cause for celebration, but Betsy and I had been in school together, and Michael and Roger sometimes worked together, so it didn't feel right to refuse.

"Lucy and Carl are coming, too," Betsy said.

"Wonderful. I get to watch while Lucy attacks Michael."

She laughed. "She is pretty blatant about it. Does he mind?"

"Mind? The last time we saw her, she kissed him on the mouth while he was getting in the car. He asked me if he could get AIDS that way. Of course, he minds. So do I," I added.

There really was something indecent about the way Lucy, in a wide-eyed and innocent way, climbed all over my husband who was too polite to call attention to the fact of her attempts at seduction. Her husband, Carl, never seemed to notice. But then he was always too busy thinking about selling furniture. He owns one of those stores that's always having a sale, the kind that advertises on TV: "Prices slashed! No down payment! No payment of any kind until . . . !"

Lucy is a failed painter turned decorator who wangled a contract with Roger to do the display models of the houses he builds, and you'd think that, and the fact that she has a perfectly decent, albeit boring husband, would be enough. But it isn't. She wants my husband, too.

"Where do you think she gets all that energy?" I asked Betsy. "And how come she hasn't put the make on Roger? Or has she?"

I could almost see Betsy's eyes roll. "I don't know to both questions. Maybe Roger isn't her type."

"Lucky you. What time does the mating dance begin?"

"Sevenish. We can eat and then sit on the terrace and watch the meteors."

"You mean the fireworks," I said, and hung up.

I usually forget about the annual arrival of the Perseid Meteors, or, if I remember, the sky is overcast because of our summer rains, but I saw them once just before Michael and I married. We sat out in the desert on the tailgate of his truck, and drank beer, and kissed, and watched the stars falling — so many stars it seemed they made a noise like thunder. I said I thought we were being blessed by heaven, and Michael agreed. We were romantics then, and still are, and we're still in love after fifteen years of marriage, some kind of a record. That's why I wished Lucy would fix her sights elsewhere. And, besides, it's hard watching a woman crawl all over your husband with only one intention in mind, especially a woman who is — or was —your friend.

Was I jealous? No. What really disturbed me was watching her make a fool of herself and, indirectly, of Michael. And for what reason? Did she really expect him to respond with the passion necessary to begin and continue a love affair? Was she really that desperate, or was she simply trying to one-up me in a way that should have gone out when we left high school?

I didn't know any of the answers, but what I suspected was that Lucy, failed painter, was jealous of me the successful novelist. Rumors came back to me, now and then, that she couldn't understand how I managed to sell my novels while she could never find a gallery that would handle her paintings.

I knew the answer, and so, probably did she. Lucy can't paint. She wants to, but wanting isn't enough. So, in the devious way of jealousy, she decided to have her revenge by stealing Michael. Why should Izzy have it all?

When I told Michael about the party, he said — "I suppose we have to go." — sounding about as happy as a French nobleman on the way to the guillotine.

"We don't *have* to," I said.

"We do. Roger wants me to do the landscaping. He called me this morning. Just don't let that woman near me."

"I could make you a chastity belt."

"Not me! She needs a straitjacket."

"What a great idea," I said. "Let's go outside, have a drink, and commune with nature."

Because of Michael's gardening talent, our acre is the culmination of his expertise and imagination, and the patio is a flowered, vine-shaded place for dreaming. From where we sat, it was hard to believe there were serpents in paradise.

"Who needs people?" Michael asked, stretching out in his chair.

"Not me. Not us. It's a shame about that development, even if you are going to do it."

He sighed and closed his eyes. "I can't stop progress. All I can do is try to disguise the mess the bulldozers make, and make sure nobody comes and plants the wrong things. I keep thinking that when everything dries up and blows away, maybe what I planted will survive."

Beside me, a hummingbird was dipping into a scarlet bougainvillea. Under the palo verde trees, the little doves pecked and wandered on pink feet, stopping now and then to give a mournful *co-o-o* as if they were commiserating with us.

"Everything used to be so simple," I said.

He sighed again. "Maybe we were just naïve."

"We knew what was important."

"Let me tell you about how Missus Bettancourt demanded a saguaro cactus put in by her garage," he said.

It seems everybody wants one of them, like

a token that they've arrived in the desert. "I'm all ears," I said.

"Well, I tried to tell her that I couldn't just go out and dig one up. That it's illegal, and she'd have to wait. So then she said that yesterday some guy came around with one on the back of his truck. Her neighbor beat her to it, so now she simply has to have one of her own."

"Think it'll live?" I asked, knowing how fragile cactus life can be.

"I don't know. It's standing next door, looking damned sorry, and I'm not a miracle worker."

"To me you are. Look what you've done here."

"This is for us," he said, and reached over and took my hand. "Besides, all I did was work with what was here the way I like to do."

I said — "I love you." — and meant it.

We were late getting to the party. Mrs. Bettancourt phoned to say she couldn't decide where she wanted the oleanders, or even, now that they'd been purchased, if she wanted oleanders at all. So poisonous!

"It's not like I didn't tell her!" Michael shouted from the shower. "I did. And then she went out and adopted a cat and says she has to protect it. What about me? I ought to charge her double."

"You're too nice," I shouted back over the rush of water.

My own afternoon hadn't gone too well, either. The chapter I was supposed to be writing ended up in the wastebasket. I kept seeing Lucy's little cat face, like a spoiled child snooping in the Christmas presents.

"Nice!" Michael exclaimed, toweling his hair. "Nice! Just try me!"

I looked at him — tanned, fresh as a flower, all male. "I'd love to."

His eyes crinkled. "Do we *have* to go tonight?"

"We can be late," I said.

"Disarmed," he said, as we drove up the twisting road toward the foothills. "Did you do that on purpose?"

"Of course not!" How could he think I was so devious? But perhaps I was. Perhaps in the swamp of my unconscious I was fighting Lucy with what I figured was the most potent weapon I had. My body.

"Well, maybe," I said. "Does it matter?"

" 'Mine is not to reason why,' mine simply to enjoy a good thing." He reached across and patted my leg. "And you, Izzy, are a good thing."

"That sounds awful."

"It was a compliment."

I knew that. After fifteen years I could tell his compliments when I heard them.

"Do you think this new development of Roger's is a good thing?" I asked, changing the subject back to what was bothering me even more than Lucy.

He shook his head. "I don't like it any more than you do, but if he doesn't do it, somebody else will. Hell, I spent half my life as a kid in that cañon! If you think it doesn't rile me, guess again."

I squirmed against the seat belt, hating the restraint. "Then isn't working with him sort of like colluding with the enemy? Like giving in?"

In answer, he stepped on the gas. "I'm not a coward, Izzy," he said, his voice flat and filled with anger.

"That's not what I meant."

"It sure sounded like it." He was going fifty-five in a twenty-five mile zone.

"Slow down and stop trying to scare me. Drive like a person," I said, picking on the one thing sure to start a fight. His — or any man's — driving.

He slammed on the brakes. "I know what I'm doing. I just don't think you do. What do you want? For me to turn down a big job? Let Devine take over with his blue grass lawns and maple trees? God dammit, I'm trying to restore, and you sit there like Buddha and tell me I'm guilty."

"Let's go home," I said.

He accelerated. "Too late. Too late for a lot of things, if you ask me."

Lucy got to the door ahead of our hosts. "Look who's here!" she announced. "We thought you forgot about us!"

"Never!" Michael beamed down on her, and I didn't know which of them I wanted to kick. "We've been thinking about you for days."

Betsy and I hugged. "I need a drink," I whispered.

"Now, now. I want you to meet some people. They just love your books and got all excited when they heard you'd be here."

"An ego trip. I need one," I said, looking around the room.

Melanie Dodson had dissatisfaction written all over her. I knew what she was going to say before she opened her mouth. That I had written just for her. That I understood her deepest yearnings. That I had changed her life.

"I hope not," I said.

She looked startled. "You do?"

"Yes, because life's hard and we have to live it. Romance is one thing. Reality is something else." I couldn't believe my ears. Where was I coming from?

Melanie's tight little lips formed an O, and made me feel mean, which I never am with fans. The blame lay with Lucy, who had her arm around Michael's waist like she owned him, and with Michael himself, who was grinning like an ape.

"I'm happy you like my books," I said gently. "They're written from the heart."

Melanie clasped her hands, perplexity replaced by idolatry. "I can tell. Women can always tell about things like that. It's men who don't understand."

Discussing the balancing act that goes on between the sexes was the last thing I wanted. I muttered something and excused myself, feeling as if I was in a gathering of strangers, people I couldn't know, and who couldn't know me, one of whom was my husband. It was as close to panic as I've ever come.

I headed through the French doors to the great room where Betsy always had her bar and her famous buffet. Flowers and vines wreathed platters of shrimp, *taquitos,* and *quesadillas,* pottery bowls overflowed with exotic fruit and salsas, *frijoles* and tiny vegetables. Martha Stewart could have learned something.

I grabbed a glass of champagne, drank it, and took another.

"Great food!" A man who looked like my hairdresser, complete with earrings, but who probably was one of Lucy's decorator flunkies, was alternately loading his plate and his mouth.

"What do you do?" he asked around the tail of a shrimp.

"Nothing," I said, and walked over to the model of Roger's latest coup that was displayed on a table beneath a computer image of the same project. It was complete, even to the cactus-studded mountains rising at the edge, those same cacti that had caused the original controversy over the development.

"What do you think?" Roger held his glass high, ready to toast himself. "A hundred acres, ninety houses. Everybody gets their own piece of desert for somewhere in the high three hundreds. And Michael's doing the landscaping. For a neat piece of change, too. So, here's to us!" He raised his glass higher.

Was I going to drink to the rape of the desert that I loved like I loved my own life? Was I supposed to fake elation while seeing quite clearly that we were victims of an enormous, earth-scouring greed? The vision of the hairdresser with shrimp sticking out of his mouth seemed particularly appropriate.

And there stood Roger, his chest puffed out like a pigeon's, and at the other end of the display Lucy and Michael were arguing the merits of various cacti, except Lucy didn't give a damn about cacti unless Michael suddenly sprouted thorns.

I raised my glass. "Here's to the rape," I said.

Roger's eyes popped. "What the hell does that mean?"

I took a deep breath. "It means that I detest this whole project. It means I can remember when I could ride all day on that hundred acres of yours and not see a person. Or a car. Or pollution. It means you can't turn the desert into a spa because sooner or later it'll turn on you and your developments, and those fake adobe houses you're so proud of. And," I added with a flourish, "it means I'm drunk."

He was angry but controlled himself. "You're never drunk. You meant it. Good to know what you think about me. But let me tell you, if it wasn't for people like me this town would still be a pathetic little pueblo lost in the Nineteenth Century."

And, oh, how I'd loved it when it was! I'd loved the small-town ambience, being able to walk where I wanted, ride out without coming across garbage dumps in the desert, or sit on the bank of the river that still had running water. That brought me to my next gripe.

"We had water to drink. Remember?"

"Don't start on that!" His face was getting red. "That's all you desert rats can think about."

No one had ever called me a desert rat before, but I kind of liked it. "That's OK," I said. "I guess, when it comes to it, we'll just have to eat cake."

The sarcasm went over his head. Roger hasn't read anything but his bank statement in years. Sometimes I wonder how Betsy stands him.

"Does Michael agree with you?" he asked.

No matter how I answered him, I'd be in trouble. Divorces have happened over less, and I didn't want a divorce. In spite of our quarrel, Michael and I were sewn together with fine stitching, like a good book or a quilt made over the years that kept us warm.

"Ask him," I said. "If you can get a word in edgewise."

At that he looked across the room and saw Lucy plastering herself to my husband. "She *is* a problem," he said.

"At least we agree on that."

He sighed. "It takes imagination to do what I do. I'd think you of all people could appreciate it.

Think of the desert as an empty page where I build dream houses like you write books. I make people happy by giving them what they want."

It was, I had to admit, a superb piece of rationalization. Roger the good. Roger as Santa Claus.

"Clever of you," I said.

He beamed. "I knew you'd see it that way. You're too smart to be a tree-hugger, Izzy. Or a desert rat, either. Oh . . . ," he broke off. "There's Wally. I need to talk to him about underground power lines. Excuse me, will you?"

Over Lucy's blonde, frizzed head — why *do* women think hair like a wet mop is attractive? — Michael shot me a look that was either warning or supplication, and I ignored it. Instead, I went out onto the terrace, Betsy's pride and joy, courtesy of Roger, another dream house constructed by the sweat of a hundred illegal workers before we cracked down on the Mexican border.

It was night. Below me the lights of the city winked through the haze, millions of lights of all colors, and on the freeway cars formed a moving, glittering necklace, while overhead a 727 began its descent.

Quite clearly I could remember how once night had claimed the desert as its own, and how it had come alive with hunting coyotes, javelinas, the great wings of owls, and once in a while the scream of a lion like a woman in pain.

At least, there weren't any houses on the mountains that jutted behind, black on a blacker sky that dazzled with stars. At some time in history, people believed that the sky was velvet and that there were small holes in the cloth, the stars the light of God shining through. How simple life must have been then! I pictured God peering down and watching us act out the comedy He'd let loose. He was, I was sure, laughing at all of us, lost souls, fools.

There were chairs in a far corner of the terrace where lemon trees heavy with fruit rustled and filled the air with the bittersweet scent of citrus. Water spouted into the pool from the mouth of a stone gargoyle, and the sound was restful. I sat down, and it seemed as if I was looking at the party-goers who clustered around the buffet like moths around a lamp, through a silken screen, far away from their voices, demands, desires.

The first meteor caught me by surprise, a trail of silver, a rent in the velvet quickly repaired. It was followed by another and another, pure light that fell like water, burned like fire, turned to ash in the infinity of sky.

These meteors were named for Perseus who, aided by Minerva's war shield and the winged shoes of Mercury, beheaded the Gorgon Medusa. Then, fleet-footed, he crossed the sky in search of adventure. I wished he would come to the party. I wished he would dance around Lucy, deflecting her sexuality with his shield before cutting off her Medusa-like head. I wished a meteor would crash into Roger's project leaving a hole two hundred yards across. And most of all I wished Michael were with me, watching the plummeting objects, some like birds with glowing tail feathers, others diamonds flung from a height I couldn't imagine.

I watched and, in the watching, saw all of us dwarfed by a galaxy and its miracle, saw us as poor, hungry beings grasping at other puny creatures in the hope of filling an unfillable emptiness. Time, as we knew it, was only a moment. Earth and space were infinite.

"Michael!" I called across the pool, through the silken screen. "Michael!"

"Izzy?"

"Come see what you're missing!"

He came toward me, almost running, and I suppressed a laugh.

"What?" he asked.

I pointed skyward. "Look up there."

A meteor as big as a cannonball plunged across, leaving a trail so brilliant that the peaks of the mountains gleamed white as bone.

"Let's not argue any more," I said. "There's so little time."

He let out a breath. "Let's go home."

"What are you two lovebirds doing?" Lucy stood, head cocked, playing sweet child and nearly succeeding except that her eyes glittered like a snake's.

Michael reached for my hand. "I'm going home and make love to my wife," he said slowly and distinctly as if Lucy were deaf.

"How quaint," she said after a second.

I laughed. "You sound like somebody out of

Jane Austen."

"You," she said, her voice thin and bitter, "what do you know?"

Michael answered for me. "She knows I love her, regardless."

"It isn't fair," she whispered. "Nothing is. Why should she have it all?"

I thought of days past when we'd been friends consoling each other, babying each other out of depression, the *Angst* of ended love affairs. I tried to pull away from Michael, but he held tight.

"Lucy needs to sit out here and watch the stars. And think," he said.

She didn't answer, and he led me out the gate.

"Why shouldn't I talk to her?" I demanded.

"Because she wouldn't listen. Let the stars fall. You can't stop them, and you can't change her, just like neither of us can stop progress. All we can do is our best, such as it is. Tomorrow, she'll be after some other poor bastard. Best pay attention to yourself. To me, because we're all we have."

That sounded as mournful as a funeral dirge, like we were locked inside our bodies unable to get out or to let anyone in.

"But . . . ," I began.

"No. Look at it this way. I plant things and watch them grow. A plant doesn't ask for anything but what nature gives it. Water. Sun. Nourishment. Unless it's mistletoe feeding off something alive. Lucy's like mistletoe. It's a sickness. People aren't supposed to suck out the life of others, but some of them do because they don't have anything inside."

I looked at the sky again, thinking that we all walked a fine line, and that even our most precious relationships could be damaged in the moment that it took a star to fall.

"Do you think earth can take care of itself?" I asked.

He nodded and, still holding my hand, pulled me over to the tailgate of the SUV. "What I think," he said slowly, "is that earth doesn't need us. We live on it, build on it, desecrate it, and none of that matters. Earth has its own set of rules, and we can't second guess it."

"Or know when it decides to get even," I said.

"That, too."

I thought back to the moment on the patio when I had, briefly, understood the concept of infinity. There was a comfort in the knowledge, a warmth in the discovery that somewhere a purpose existed, whether or not it was discernable.

"Let's get a six pack and go up the cañon," I said.

He grinned. "You mean like drink a toast to the desert?"

"And to us while we're at it."

"Let's go." He held open the door, and I climbed inside.

Over our heads a rain of stars began, and I thought I could hear them — falling shards, tears of the ancients, laughter of the desert gods.

Rodeo

When Nolo Pearce woke up, he was in the Fort Worth hospital with his foot in a cast, seven broken ribs, and a concussion. The first thing he saw was his wife, Noreen, staring at him out of expressionless black eyes.

"You're awake," she said.

"Reckon so. What happened? Last I remember, I was coming out of the chute on that Accelerator horse."

"You came out, all right. That bronc' tried to stomp you. I thought you were dead."

Nolo's head hurt, and his vision was blurred, but he grinned at her. "Honey, it'd take more than one loco bronc' to kill me."

"That's what they all say." She blew her nose on a tissue. "How do you think I felt, watching them carry you out on a stretcher? I'm too young to be a widow, that's how I felt. Like I got cheated."

Nolo frowned, trying to make sense out of what she was saying, but he couldn't seem to concentrate. Finally he asked: "Cheated how?"

"Out of half my life, that's how. Out of all the things we were going to do, you and me." She blew her nose again and looked at him, and for one crazy second she reminded him of a rattle-snake.

"Honey. . . ."

She cut him off. "Don't honey me. I made up my mind on my way here, following that ambulance. I'm leaving you, and I'm taking Cody with me. I'm tired of being a tag-along rodeo wife, holding my breath every time you go out there, waiting to see you get your neck broke. I'm tired not having anything. I deserve better, and I'm going to get it. And you won't stop me because you can't."

That was true. His ribs jabbed every time he moved, and his head ached like thunder. "Can't we talk about this tomorrow?"

"I won't be here tomorrow." She stood up, bent down, and kissed him on the forehead.

Like he was a kid, he thought with a surge of anger. Like he was being put to bed with a pat and a kiss and a — "Be a good boy." — as if he had nothing to say in the matter.

Well, his foot and ribs might be busted, but his hands still worked. He reached out and grabbed her wrist, and was pleased when she winced. "Don't you take my boy," he said.

"He's mine, too. I'm the one that had him." She tried to twist away, but couldn't break his grip.

"You hear what I said, Noreen? You take Cody, and it'll be the sorriest day of your life."

"Don't threaten me!" Her teeth showed white against her red lipstick. "The sorriest day I ever had was the day I met you. Now let go!" She threw all her weight back, and he released her with a groan.

"Don't do it, Noreen."

"Like I said, you can't stop me." She picked up her purse and walked out without looking back.

Nolo's first impulse was to catch her before she got away, but he had no clothes except the ridiculous hospital gown, and his ribs protested as he made a sudden move.

There was no doubt she meant what she said. She'd always been headstrong and a little spoiled, but he'd liked that about her — liked being kept on the edge, and the way her dark eyes mirrored her moods, all of them, even the angry ones. Except this time she hadn't been angry, just determined.

Cody! The pain in his heart at the thought of losing his son was worse than the jab of his ribs. He had to stop her. Had to! He pressed the button beside the bed to call the nurse, and, when he'd gotten no response for several minutes, he opened his mouth and bellowed: "Nurse!"

Within seconds, a gray-haired woman bustled in. "Mister Pearce," she said, assessing his posture as he hunched on the edge of the bed, "please, Mister Pearce, lower your voice. This is a hospital."

"I know what it is, and I want out of here," Nolo said. "Where's my clothes?"

She shook a finger at him, making him feel

once again like a schoolboy. "Get back into bed. You can't leave till doctor says. And as for your clothes, they're probably in the incinerator."

"You don't understand. . . ."

How could she? How could this woman know about his problems: that his wife was running out on him with a four year old calling for his daddy, and his daddy helpless, dressed in a white gown that was three sizes too small?

"You had a concussion, Mister Pearce." Expertly she guided him back into bed. "And broken bones and contusions. If you're in pain, I can get you something, but you've got to stay in bed and stop shouting."

He leaned back and closed his eyes. "How soon can I leave?"

"When doctor says. And there's somebody outside who's been waiting to see you."

"Who?"

"A man named Bevins."

Nolo allowed himself a smirk. Merle Bevins would help him. "Let him in," he said.

"Only if you promise to behave. None of your cowboy tricks." She peered at him over her glasses.

"Cross my heart."

"Yes . . . well," she said, and left the room at a silent trot.

Merle Bevins had been a father and a friend since Nolo started on the rodeo circuit. He had taught Nolo everything he knew, which was plenty, and he'd stood up at the wedding when

Nolo married Noreen, although he had his doubts about her as a wife.

"That gal's a handful," he'd warned. "Never been broke right."

But Nolo was young and sure of himself. He'd wanted Noreen and was going to have her come hell or high water. And look where that had got him. He pounded his fist on the sheet.

Merle came in and stood at the end of the bed. "Thought you was a goner."

"Hell, it'd take more than one mean horse to bury me."

Merle shook his head. "You were lucky, and that's the truth. That horse was a man-eater. Went after you like you was a snake." He shook his head again, as if trying to erase the image. "I saw Noreen in the hall lookin' like she had a lit fuse under her tail. What's goin' on?"

"She says she's leaving and taking Cody. You got to help me stop her."

"Nobody ever stopped Noreen with her mind made up," Merle said. Then he read the anguish in Nolo's eyes. "She sure picked her time, didn't she?"

"Go after her. And get me some clothes so I can get out of here." Nolo's voice cracked. "A boy needs his daddy, Merle. I made a promise to myself that I'd be a good one to Cody, and I don't break promises."

Merle knew. He'd watched Nolo grow from a gawky teenager into manhood, from a fatherless kid with a no-good mother into this man trapped in a hospital bed desperate to save what needed saving.

Merle had never liked Noreen. In his opinion she was grasping and selfish, out for what she could get. But Cody, well, Cody was his dad all over, without the scars of a rough childhood. Not yet, anyhow. Damn the woman!

He slammed his hat onto his gray head. "Rest easy. I'll do what I can."

"And get me out of here."

"That, too."

Merle pulled up in the space where Nolo's truck and trailer had been parked.

"Huh!" he said to himself. "Just like her to haul ass and not waste any time about it." He hunched over the steering wheel and stared off, thinking about where she'd go, what she'd do now that she considered herself a free woman. What he came up with wasn't pretty, but, if they could get the boy, they'd be well rid of his mother.

"Damn your hide, woman," he muttered. "You'll be glad to see the last of us when we're done with you."

Then he turned his truck and headed for a store that sold jeans, boots, shirts, and underwear, because for sure Nolo wasn't escaping that place in a piece of cloth that barely kept him decent.

"She's gone," he said, standing there holding

two shopping bags and unable to meet Nolo's eyes. "Took your truck and trailer, too."

Nolo's face twisted. "I should've known. But we'll find her. Find her and fight it out. Whatever it takes."

Merle tossed the jeans and shirt on the bed. "You bet," he said. "Now let's get going."

Getting going took a while. Nolo was no stranger to broken bones, but putting his arms into sleeves was an exercise in heroics. "I'm not taking this mother off till I got to," he muttered through his teeth. "Even if I get to stinkin'."

"You do, I'll shove you under a shower. You be all right walking in that cast?"

He'd walk. He'd walk a hundred miles to get to Cody. But in what direction? "Where'd you think she went?" he asked.

"I been studyin' that one. I figure she went home to Mama. Or else to her sister's. She'll want a place to park the kid so she can go kick up her heels."

Nolo groaned. Noreen wouldn't have any trouble picking up boy friends, but, if she brought them around Cody, he'd kill her with his own two hands. "Her mother doesn't like me," he said.

"She don't have to. All she's got to do is listen to reason. And how about the sister? I only met her that once, but she seemed OK."

"Karla's different. She said Noreen was always stealing her boy friends, so there's no love lost between them."

Merle nodded. "I believe it. You ready?"

Nolo unfolded his six feet, two slowly. "Yeah. Let's hit it."

Afterwards, he knew he'd tell the story about his exit from the hospital with the nurses scolding and running like jack rabbits up and down the hall. It was almost but not quite funny, all those women in a panic just because of him.

Once in Merle's truck, he laughed, a short laugh because it hurt. "I'm never goin' to a hospital again. All that fuss . . . like I was dying or something. Hell, I busted ribs before and lived to do it all over again."

Merle revved the engine, cocked his head to listen to the sounds under the hood. His truck was old, and he didn't want any trouble on the road. "I know folks that purely love hospitals. It's how they get attention."

"Sick," Nolo said.

"Yeah, but not in a way a doctor's gonna help." Satisfied with the truck, he shifted into gear. "Which way?"

"Back the way we came."

Nolo watched the road a while, hoping he'd catch sight of Noreen and his rig, but she had a head start and had always driven like a bat out of hell. Finally he put his head back and closed his eyes.

Sleep didn't come. What came were images of Cody — in the hospital after his birth, taking his first faltering steps, proudly showing off a pair of fancy red boots — "Like Daddy's." — astride Nolo's big gelding, Tucker, looking like he'd been born there. And Noreen, *his* Noreen, moving around the little house on the ranch where he worked as wrangler, lying in his arms at night while they dreamed of the ranch they'd buy someday.

He opened his eyes and stared at the road again. In the hospital she'd acted like she hated him, but he'd never seen signs of it before. She had simply always been there, his wife, his woman. And if sometimes she turned sulky, well, he couldn't blame her. She was young, younger than he could ever remember being himself, and not used to doing without the things she thought she should have. Nothing made sense, at least nothing he could grasp. He could understand her fear, but not her desire to hurt him, to cut him off from his life and his child.

"I can't figure it," he said to Merle. "I keep trying, but I can't."

Merle took his time answering. The kid was hurting inside and out, and he hated making it worse, but he also hated covering up what he saw as the truth. "Tell you what," he said slowly. "That gal always wants what she don't have. There's lots like her, you stop to think on it. She got you, and then you weren't enough. That wasn't your fault. She's like a horse always lookin' at the grass over the fence. You're well rid of her, if you'll pardon me sayin' so."

"But I love her," Nolo said.

"There's all kinds of love, just like there's different people." He shot a glance at Nolo out of the corner of his eye. "And there's lots of women in this world, some better, some worse. Take it from me."

"You never been married." Nolo fished on the dash for a cigarette.

"You don't know everything," Merle shot back. "I been married twice. The first run off, just like Noreen. Marnie . . . well, she was different. She died just before you come along."

Nolo heard the loneliness in his friend's voice. "I'm sorry."

"Yeah." Merle concentrated on passing a semi. "Things happen."

"Think I'll get Cody?"

"I'd say so. You sure you ought to be smokin' that?"

"It passes the time."

Nolo felt miserable, for himself and for Merle who'd lived since he'd known him in a trailer outside town — an old man's life with his Blue Heeler dog and a roping horse so ancient Merle had to grind up its feed.

He could picture himself, an old cowboy bent over from too many broken bones, without Noreen, without Cody or anybody to care for or to care for him, and the hopelessness of it all stuck in his throat like a stone.

"Karla's place is between here and her mom's," he said. "Let's stop there. She might've heard something."

Karla was out on her porch to meet them, a shotgun in her hands.

"Holy hell!" Merle exclaimed.

Nolo rolled down the window and stuck out his head. "Hey, Karla! It's me. Nolo. Put that thing down." To Merle he said: "Her husband died last year. Guess she's not taking any chances."

"Smart woman." Merle peered through the windshield and nodded approval. "I always admired a woman who could look after herself."

Karla watched, frowning as Nolo eased himself out of the truck. "What happened to you?" she asked.

"Everything."

"You want help getting up the steps?"

He shook his head. "It's better if I just do it myself. You remember Merle?"

"I sure do." She turned and smiled, and her blue eyes crinkled at the corners. "Both of you come on in. The coffee's hot."

When they were seated around the old oak table in the kitchen, she leaned her chin in her hands and looked from one to the other. "Who's going to tell me what's going on?"

They told her together and watched the smile fade from her face. She sat, saying nothing, drawing idle circles on the scarred oak surface. When she looked up, her eyes were sad.

"To tell the truth," she said, "I wondered if this would happen."

"How come?"

"Noreen was the baby in the family. After Dad died, we all kind of spoiled her. She . . . she's like some butterfly. Always was, even then. Just going from one flower to another without thinking." Karla reached out and took a cigarette from Nolo's pack. "I figured you'd get hurt, but it wasn't my place to say anything. And, anyhow, you wouldn't have listened."

Nolo sighed. "So everybody knew I was making a mistake but me."

"I figured you had a chance, if anybody did. And when Cody came, well, hell, I thought you were a real family, and maybe that's what she needed." Karla lit the cigarette, inhaled deeply, and blew out smoke that hovered in the air over their heads. "Maybe," she said at last, "maybe she *can't* settle. There's women who can't. Her running off is one thing. Taking Cody . . . that was bad of her."

The morning sun came through the window and made a halo around Karla's head, and Nolo thought how different she was from her sister, with her reddish hair tied in a ponytail, and the concern in her eyes that slanted above high cheek bones. He couldn't remember that Noreen had ever been concerned for anybody except herself, not even for Cody.

"I'd let her go if that's what she wants," he said. "As long as she leaves Cody with me."

"I bet she's on her way to Mom's," Karla said. "And if I know Mom, she doesn't want another kid to raise, so I'll tell you what. I'll get him for you. He'll be better off with you."

"How?"

She grinned. "Easy. I'll just show up, take him out for an ice cream, and skedaddle. Meet you up at the truck stop on the Interstate."

"Think it'll work?" he asked, trying to visualize the kidnapping.

"Don't be stupid. Of course, it'll work." She got up and cleared the table. "You guys rest a while. I've got some chores to do."

Merle followed her out and stood on the porch, admiring the well kept yard and barn. "You do a good job," he said.

"Thanks. I try."

"It shows." He thought about how pleasant it would be to live there in the broad valley with its grass and scattered trees, mountains rising gently to east and west, and the only sound the song of the wind humming through a wire fence. A good place to grow up, he decided. A good place to grow old.

"You here by yourself?" he asked.

She snorted. "Not hardly. There's too much work for just me. Fidencio and Tony were here when I came, and they stayed on after . . . after Joe died." Her voice faltered.

Damn! Now he'd upset her, the last thing he intended. He scuffed the heel of his boot in the dust. "I'm sorry about that. Nolo told me."

"It's all right," she said. "Really."

"Always stickin' my foot in my mouth." He watched a family of quail pecking in the dust so

251

he wouldn't have to look at her as he asked his next question. "What do you think Nolo oughta do after we get Cody?"

The abrupt change of subject surprised her. "I don't know. Take him home, I guess."

"Yeah. But that place is only Nolo's long as he's working for the Flying D. He ain't gonna be working for six weeks or more."

"Oh." Her face was blank. "Nothing's easy, is it?"

"Not that I ever noticed."

"Damn Noreen!" She kicked a stone out of the path, and the quail scattered and flew. "She's my sister, but she's no good and never was. Always breaking every damn' thing she touched. Including people. I'll tell you what. . . ." Her eyes glittered, and her cheek bones seemed ready to poke through her skin, and Merle thought there was an Indian ancestress somewhere not too far back — a fighting woman, one to be wary of. "I'll tell you what. You and Nolo and Cody can stay here. Long as you like. Anyway, it's a cinch she'll come after him, and, when she does, we'll be waiting. The four of us. That puts the odds in our favor."

Merle grinned at her. "Count me in. There's a few things I always wanted to tell that little gal."

"Me, too," Karla said. "Oh, me, too."

"I don't know," Nolo said when they informed him of their plan. "People are gonna talk, us living here with you."

"And I don't give a hoot what people say." Karla's chin jutted out. "You're in no shape to go any place, and I've got room. Besides, Cody knows me. We get along."

It seemed his mind was being made up for him, as usual, and he thought about that, about things happening to him over which he had no warning and no control. His whole life had been a series of incidents for which he'd been unprepared, like a dream — or in this case a nightmare — that didn't end, just got more complicated with every day.

Karla was a good woman. He admired how she'd stuck it out after Joe died, running the ranch as well as any man, avoiding situations that caused talk. And now here he was putting her smack in the middle of a scandal and not much he could do about it.

"I never meant to cause you trouble," he said.

She gave him a severe look. "It's not your fault."

"Maybe it is."

As if she read his mind, she said: "You didn't start this. My sister did. The way I see it, we've got to play with the cards we're holding. Either that or quit and miss the good times as well as the bad ones."

"The good times are lookin' mighty scarce right now," he said.

The telephone rang, and Karla jumped up. "Bet it's Mom who just got a surprise."

When she came back after a long time, her face was grim.

"What?" both men asked in unison.

She sat down on the porch step. "Noreen's there all right, and Cody's with her. But it seems she took a little detour down to the Flying D. Told them you weren't coming back, and cleaned out the house."

"Hell!" Nolo said. "My stuff, too? My trophies and saddle and all?"

"Looks like it."

"I'm back where I started. With the clothes on my back." He couldn't believe it, couldn't understand her reasons unless, for a fact, she hated him. "Why'd she do that?"

"Because that's how she is," Karla answered, her tone containing a hint of irritation.

"Don't get mad," Nolo said.

"I'm not. I just think you got handed a lesson, and you'd better study on it hard. There's more."

"Now what?"

"She told Cody you weren't ever coming back, too."

He sat up straight in his chair, winced, then cursed a blue streak. "I'll wring her little neck," he said when he'd calmed down. "He's probably scared to death, and she ain't making it any easier. When are we going? We got to save my boy."

She leaned over and put a hand over his. "Easy," she said. "Easy now," like she was talking to a spooked horse. "Let's wait a couple days till you feel better. It won't make any difference in the long run, and Noreen won't be looking for you every time a car goes down the road. OK?"

"Makes sense to me," Merle said.

Frankly, nothing made sense to Nolo, but he nodded agreement. That night he spent on the couch, his foot propped on the coffee table, his ribs on fire, his head aching. Sleep wouldn't come, so he thought, or tried to think, about what had gone wrong and why, but when morning came, all he could figure was that he, Nolo Pearce, was what was generally called a damned fool, taken in by a pretty woman just like every country music song he'd ever heard. His trouble was, he'd never paid any attention to the words, just hummed along while he went about his business, figuring he was immune.

He'd been blinded, at first by Noreen's hero-worship act, then by her looks and the way she acted in bed — like she'd never get enough of him, and him so wonderful. "Just a calf to the slaughterhouse," he muttered to himself. "That was me." It didn't make him feel any better.

⸱ "Now this'll take me some time, so you guys be patient. Read the paper or something." The three conspirators were sitting in a booth at the truck stop, Nolo uncomfortable, his leg out in the aisle.

"I can't stay like this all day," he said.

"You just think about Cody, and let me do what I have to." Karla stood up and smoothed her skirt over her hips, an unconscious gesture that drew Nolo's attention in spite of his promises to himself the night before.

She was, he realized, a damned fine-looking woman, and honest to boot. He wondered how she and Noreen had come out of the same litter, but decided not to ask.

"Good luck," he said instead, and watched her out the door, her flowered skirt swirling around her.

"How d'you suppose that old woman threw such different pups?" he asked Merle when she'd gone.

Merle chuckled. "That old woman was as wild as Noreen in her day. No tellin' who the daddies were."

"Geez." Nolo fell silent, thankful that Cody was his mirror image. No room for doubt there, at least.

His own mother hadn't been much better, but, at least, he'd known his own daddy. It was only after his death that his mother had gotten restless and started moving from town to town, man to man, dragging him along like so much unwanted baggage, like Noreen might do with Cody, given time.

"Women," he said. "You can never tell what they'll do next."

Merle chuckled like he knew a joke he hadn't told yet. "That depends on the woman."

"I'm never depending on a woman again," Nolo said. "Count on it."

"Son, you're doin' just that right now."

Nolo looked at him in amazement. "Well, god-damn," he said.

Karla cruised past her mother's house in low gear. Parked to one side was Nolo's stolen trailer, a tricycle overturned beside it. The truck was nowhere in sight. "Making it easy for me, aren't you, little sis?" she said out loud. In the last year she'd started talking to herself to fill the silence. Now it had become habit, but one she was comfortable with. If she was a little cracked, there wasn't anybody on the ranch to comment or care.

Her mother, Lucille, came to the door. "I thought you were Noreen come back early."

"Just me, Mom." She gave Lucille a peck on the cheek. "Where'd she go?"

Lucille shrugged. "Off to a barbecue and a roping with Sandy Mullin."

"He's married," Karla said.

Lucille giggled. "He doesn't think so."

"Noreen's not wasting any time obviously."

"Now you know how she is," Lucille said. "She's just young and full of life."

"And old enough to know better."

Karla followed her mother into the kitchen. Dirty dishes were piled in the sink, and the remains of lunch sat on the table.

"Where's Cody?"

Lucille sat down and lit a cigarette. "Taking a nap, thank goodness. He's like to wore me out the last couple days. Asking for his daddy and bawling his head off."

Automatically Karla stacked the plates and took them to the sink. With her back turned, she asked: "You think it's right? What she did?"

"I can see she wants better than what she's got. Not as if I didn't tell her."

"There's better ways to go about it than running off like she did."

Lucille leaned back in her chair and crossed her legs. "You know Noreen's always been independent. There's no stopping her once she makes up her mind."

Karla fought the urge to laugh and scream both at once. Life was like a crazy rodeo ride, a chuck wagon race, and they were all caught up in it, careening wildly toward some finish line she couldn't see and might never reach. Where were the rules? Who were the judges? And what would be salvaged from the certainty to a wreck? Likely they'd all end up broken, like Nolo, and forced to start over until they were too old and tired to care.

Her momentary vision was shattered by Cody who ran out of the bedroom and threw his arms around her legs. "Aunty Karla!" His wail was piercing and frightened. "Aunty Karla!"

She crouched down beside him and smoothed the hair from his eyes. "Well, hi, little 'un," she said. "Got a kiss for me?"

In response, he buried his head in her shoulder, and she felt him trembling.

"Hey," she said. "That's no way to say hello. Not when I came to take you out for ice cream."

"Daddy." The word was muffled.

"Sh-h-h." Over his head she looked at Lucille. "How about I get him cleaned up and take him out for a while?"

"Go ahead. I could use a *siesta*."

"OK, cowboy." She picked him up. "Here we go."

Inside the trailer she set him down and looked around. Clothes were scattered in a random trail from the bathroom to the kitchenette, and tossed in a corner was Nolo's prize hand-made saddle, stirrups, and cinches twisted together. "Typical Noreen," she said, and at the sound Cody tugged at her skirt.

"I want Daddy."

Once again she crouched down. "I'll tell you a secret, but you can't say anything to anybody. Not even Gramma. Promise?"

He nodded, and his tear-filled eyes brightened.

"When you get dressed, you and me are going to find your daddy. OK?"

His round face, so much like Nolo's, lit in a smile. " 'K. Hurry!"

In the bathroom she found more evidence of Noreen — powder, lipstick, mascara left where they fell, and the heavy scent of Shalimar over all.

"Only your mother would wear Shalimar to a roping," she said.

But Cody wasn't interested in matters of taste. "Let's go," he prompted. "Let's go to Daddy."

She washed his hands and face and then went through the trailer shoving his clothes and extra shoes into the big purse she'd brought for the purpose. At the last minute, she stopped beside the saddle. "Well, damn!" she said. "I'm not leaving you here to rot!" She picked it up by the horn, tossed stirrups and cinches over the seat. "Come on, little 'un. We're going for a long ride."

"My horse!" Cody ran to the closet. "This is mine!" he announced proudly, hauling out a stick horse. "Mine. Like Tucker is Daddy's."

"OK. Bring him along."

He followed, clucking to his toy as if it were real and carrying him to where he wanted to go.

"What on earth do you think you're doing?" Lucille screeched through the screen. "You're taking that saddle! What for?"

Karla hefted Cody and the saddle into the truck. "It's too good to waste on Noreen, Mom. Have a good nap." She jumped in, peeled out in a screech of tires and a cloud of dust.

"We're in the getaway car," she said to Cody. "Fun, isn't it?"

He nodded, eyes wide. "Go fast. Go fast, Aunty Karla. Don't let them catch us."

Feisty little son-of-a-gun, she thought, *and deserving better than the mother who'd borne him. Oh, yes. Much better.*

With a shout of pure joy, Cody hurled himself at Nolo who put out an arm in self-defense.

"Whoa there, cowboy!"

Cody skidded to a stop. "Daddy?"

"Yep. But come easy. I'm bunged up."

Even at four, Cody, his father's son, understood. "He was sure a mean horse, wasn't he?"

"Yeah, but not meaner than me. Now give me a kiss. Easy."

Cody stood between his legs, his face shining. "Mom said you weren't never coming back."

"Guess she was wrong." Nolo felt his heart contract just looking at the boy, so full of trust and happiness. And Noreen was ready to take advantage of it, of a child. In his mind she began to take on the shape of a monster, insatiable, feeding on everybody who came near. Maybe he wasn't the world's smartest, but he knew he'd die for the boy standing there.

"How about an ice cream?" he asked, his voice unsteady.

"Strawberry," came the answer. "Please."

"We've got time," Karla said, slipping into the booth beside Merle. "Noreen went to a barbecue with Sandy Mullin."

"He's married," Nolo said.

"And Noreen's thinking big. As in big ranch, big bucks, big, fancy house."

It was too awful to think about. Inside, Nolo was still raw. He watched Cody attack his ice cream. "What now?" he asked.

"Now we go home and wait. It won't be long. Tomorrow noon would be my guess. She'll show up snorting fire."

"You don't like her much, do you?"

A wry smile twisted her mouth. "Not hardly." Not, she thought, since she'd first laid eyes on Nolo and had lost him before she ever had a chance.

They heard Noreen before they saw her. She was coming over the dirt road at a speed more suited to a four-lane highway.

"That's my truck she's beating hell out of!" Nolo said. "Jesus!"

"Better it than you," Merle put in.

The three were on the porch, waiting. Cody had been turned over to Fidencio to learn to ride the oldest horse on the place. He'd gone without complaint, smiling from ear to ear.

Noreen pulled up and jumped out, slamming the door so hard it didn't catch and swung open, but she didn't notice. Her attention was on Nolo.

"You! You son-of-a-bitch!" she shrieked. "And you, my own sister. Kidnapping my kid. Who in hell do you think you are?"

Before anybody could answer, Merle pointed a finger at her. "Why don't you just settle down and talk nice."

She turned on him. "Shut up, old man. This isn't your fight."

Unruffled, he spat a stream of tobacco juice. "I always said you was bad-mannered. That's your trouble. That and no respect for nobody. Not even your own kid."

"Don't you tell me about my kid. Where is he? If I don't get him back, I'll have you all in jail for kidnapping."

Nolo pushed himself slowly up out of his chair. "You're talkin' about Cody like he's a piece of meat instead of a child. If you got problems with me, fine, but I won't have you taking them out on him. And there'll be no more talk about jail, either. You're the one who took him first. And crossed a couple state lines, too. Reckon you haven't thought about that."

"I'm his mother."

"And I'm his daddy. And he won't ever wake up and find me out in the bushes with some stranger."

She went for him, her fingers curved into claws, but Karla stepped in between and deflected her sister with her arm.

"Get . . . out . . . of . . . my . . . way!" Noreen's face contorted. "I went out with Sandy. So what? You expect me to sit home knitting?" She aimed a slap at her sister and missed.

"Quit! Quit, I say!" Nolo shouted at the top of his lungs, and regretted it immediately.

"Make me."

"Shut up and sit. Both of you. And listen to me, or, by God, I'll snatch you bald-headed. Should've done it a long time ago and kept you home."

"Hah!" Noreen said. "Go ahead and try." But

seeing something deadly in his eyes, she took a step back.

"That's better." He stood, fishing around for the right words, hoping they'd come and not leave him looking the fool. It wasn't often he got angry, and, when he did, he went out and dug post holes, or rode up in the mountains until the anger had gone. And explaining himself to others had never come easily.

"Look at us," he said. "It's not pretty. Us screaming and jumping like a bunch of fighting cocks. Downright uncivilized, you ask me."

"You're such an authority." Noreen put her hands on her hips. "Besides, who started it?"

"You did, if I'm not mistaken. You up and left me back there. And you took everything. My truck, my trailer, my boy. And then you lost me my job and cleaned out our house. *Our* house. Not yours. As I recollect, this is a community property state. You want my stuff, that's fine. You want the money we saved. That's fine, too. All I want's Cody. You can have the rest, and good riddance."

"It's not that easy."

"Yeah, it is. 'Specially when the judge or the sheriff hears about you screwing your head off."

Noreen drew back her lips in a snarl. "Prove it!"

"It's easy enough." Karla's own anger was at the explosion point. "All we have to do is look at the record."

"Sure. And here's my husband and kid living

264

with you. That doesn't look too good, either."

"I'm chaperon," Merle said mildly. "No need to worry."

Noreen wheeled around. "I told you, this isn't your fight."

"Yeah, it is. Nolo's like my own son, and you didn't measure up. The way I see it, you never will."

Without warning, Noreen put her head back and laughed, a mocking laugh that reminded Nolo of a coyote.

"What's so damned funny?"

She gave him a black look. "You. You're all a bunch of rejects hoping to get the better of me. And just because I snatched a kid and want to better myself."

Merle had had enough. He grabbed Noreen's arm and headed her toward the steps. "Let me tell you something, little gal. You want to play rough, you'd better get a hell of a lot tougher and smarter. But you'll do it alone. And you'll do it 'cause I know what you been up to when Nolo wasn't payin' attention. I saw you with my own eyes goin' into that motel in San Antone, but I kept my mouth shut. Didn't think I oughta interfere. But no more. You ain't fit to raise that boy or any other boy. You ain't fit to raise your own self. Now you go on and get in that truck and haul yourself back to Mama. Your divorce papers'll be in the mail, and you'll sign 'm and go on about your business. Understand?"

She glared at him, her face white under the

make-up she'd never removed. "You're a dirty old man, and that's blackmail," she said through her teeth. And to Nolo: "As for you, you're a cowboy with his brains kicked out. Karla's welcome to you . . . and your brat . . . and good riddance. Maybe between the three of you, you'll amount to something someday."

Swinging her hips, she walked cross the yard to the truck. The last thing they saw was her hand out the window, one finger high in the air.

Nolo looked at Merle. "You saw her? And didn't tell me?"

Merle spat, grinned, shrugged. "I didn't exactly see her, but I figured where they were headed. Guess I was right, seein' as it sure put a burr under her tail."

"Shame on you!" But Karla was laughing. It wasn't too often that Noreen got bested.

Nolo sat down and put his head in his hands. "She was my wife. We had all these plans, and I believed she wanted them, too. But there she was, cheatin' on me the whole time."

"Was," Karla corrected. "She was your wife. But no more. That's what you got to think about."

"I'm tired thinkin'."

She guessed he was. She guessed he was tired inside and out and would be for a while. "Then don't. There's nothing so bad that time doesn't make it feel better."

"Amen." Merle hunkered down on the top step and looked off at the mountains. "And if time don't do it, why this country will, all by itself. Big as it is, it's seen everything, and it's still here. And as for us, we ain't dead, and we've got a boy to raise."

They heard Cody's laughter before they saw him, perched on top of a big white horse, reins held securely in his small fists.

"Go tell Cody how good he looks," Karla said. "I'll start lunch. Chili's cooking."

"Gal," Merle said, "if I wasn't so old, I'd ask you to marry me."

"And if I wasn't so young, I'd accept. As it is, I'll wait and take my chances." She winked, and the two of them burst into laughter.

Nolo looked from one to the other, trying to figure out the joke. Then, with a grin, he turned to Cody, his boy who hadn't yet broken his heart and maybe never would. Love was a risky business, but there were times, and this was one, when you took the chance.

"Ride him, cowboy," he said. "Ride him like I know you can."

Marvel Bird

You stand looking at the shack where you lived, where dreams were supposed to happen and didn't, and you're split in half, like in a mirror, watching yourself, Marvel Bird, saying good bye.

You go through the rooms, a thin, dark shadow, kneel to straighten the covers on the mattress that served you and Larry as a bed. You grimace as you look at it — the grimy quilt, the old pillowcases even the sun can't bleach.

"Get up! Get up!" — you want to scream at yourself, but disgust is thick in your throat. You turn your back, look out to the mountains, to the valley mottled red, yellow, dun, the hills rounded like the hips of a woman.

You were born in the valley. It is in you, and it calms the way a mother should calm, or a lover. A sweetness runs through it, pacifying you. Ever the fatalist, you shrug your shoulders. "Ah," you say, "ah," — and the sound comes out like wind in cottonwood leaves.

You water your plants a last time, standing in the middle of the porch you built with your own hands out of old two-by-fours and sheets of plastic. The plastic is ripped now, rotted by sun. You were proud of your room at first, although Larry laughed at your efforts. "What's wrong with the rooms we've got?" he kept asking. But this was your place with green things in it reaching toward light.

Life with Larry Mallory had once held such promise. A room of your own and space to grow. A pasture for the horse you were raising from colthood. No more miner's shack, a room shared with three sisters and the old Indian woman, your grandmother, who passed down to you her thick black hair, her magic with growing things.

You were sixteen, and your hair hung to your waist in a braid thick as a man's arm. You were in the patch of garden behind your father's house weeding, watering, forcing life out of the cracked earth by will. And you were listening to your dad and Larry who sat on the porch talking about the smelter closing, and your dad with eight mouths to feed.

That was the evening that Larry stopped on his way out of the yard and looked at you a long time. His eyes were blue as Grandma's turquoise *naja*. That was what you saw. Maybe that was enough.

"The rains don't come, that little bit of water won't help," he said finally.

And you said: "Can't anybody around here talk about anything but the weather? Can't anybody say something good?" Then you bit your lip, feeling tears behind your eyes, and something rising inside like bread sealed in an oven.

He pulled back at that, and his blue eyes got round. "Hey," he said. "Hey, now. I was just passin' the time."

"Go pass it some place else, then," you said, and you felt mean.

Your grandmother said: "Your tongue could cut rope."

Your mother was silent. She was always silent, as if she had no tongue at all, or no words for what she felt.

"You got no cause to speak to my friends that way." That was your dad, embarrassed because a daughter of his had a tongue like a knife.

"Him and his blue eyes and dumb talk," you said. You tossed your braid and left the house, taking the old trail out into the valley where larks rose up singing from under your feet, and the ocotillo scratched the sky with flame. They grew on each side of the trail like trees lining a street, but they cast no shade except thin shadows that criss-crossed in the dust.

"Smart mouth," you said to yourself, remembering his blue eyes under raised brows, and you let the tears come, all the way to your lips.

The next time he came, you apologized.

He said: "Hey! It was nothing. No need getting upset."

You looked at the ground and saw that his boots were worn, a chunk of leather missing from one toe.

"I got a new car," he said. "I'll take you for a ride."

You went with him up the mountain to watch the sunset. The sky and earth changed colors so fast you couldn't keep up and reached out with your hands to catch the swirling.

"You like dancing?" he asked, watching you.

The idea frightened you. "I don't know. I never tried."

"Come on, then." He sat you in the jeep and drove fast, a cloud of dust behind, drove to Obregon's Café where he bought you a beer and then another, and whirled you around the wooden dance floor till you were dizzy, light as a leaf, a dust devil touching down.

That's when you started to laugh and couldn't stop. It spilled out and over him till he laughed, too, crinkling his eyes. "You're something," he said. "You really are. Old Man Bird's daughter." He shook his head in wonder.

In the car you let him touch you, forgetting all the words of caution you'd heard, the whispers of women, the bulging shame of those who'd fallen. You looked down at your breasts in surprise as if they'd just grown there, pale in the moonlight, your hair spilling across them, a dark stream.

"Marvelous Bird," he said. "Marvelous Bird." And you laughed again deep in your throat, reached out for him as you'd reached for the falling sun.

He courted you then, promised you a house, a bed of your own with only him in it, a horse to raise and ride, free as the wind. You believed him and held on to that belief for years.

"Men are often fools," your grandmother told you. "Making promises they can't keep and babies to hold you." She told you how to stop a child from being conceived, and you listened.

Your mother said nothing, although she sewed on your wedding dress, pinned it around you, humming a song that had no melody, like the song of the wind in the fences.

For a wedding present, Larry bought you a colt, a wild-eyed spotted thing you loved like a child, like part of yourself, the part tied to earth and leaping away.

"Name him well," your grandmother said. She breathed her breath into his nostrils and spoke quietly to him, soothing his excitement.

You called him Naja after the turquoise crescent on her necklace and after Larry's eyes.

The trailer where you went to live after the wedding had three rooms, a yard filled with prickly pear, and a pasture with tall grasses for the colt to eat. You loved him. You thought you loved Larry, even when the smelter closed and he had no work. Even when he refused to look for another job and sat every day in the kitchen reading old newspapers, the television casting blue shadows across his face.

That was when you built this room for yourself, setting in two-by-fours, lining it with plastic. You filled it with plants you dug in the fields or begged from the neighbors, and you nurtured them as you nurtured Naja who followed you like a dog, let you lead him, lift his hoofs, brush his dark mane and tail.

You planted a garden, putting in long rows of

seeds in the light of the growing moon, and you bought five black hens and a cock with bronze feathers. You had your mouth to feed, and Larry's, and you did the best you could, feeling fury as you dug, wanting to crack the pale eggs in your palm. You thought about promises and lies, and your mouth curled down and stayed that way.

And you got a job exercising horses at Cy Epperson's training stable. You were unafraid on horseback, and you could steal grain for Naja who ate the strength from your hand.

"That's no job for a woman," Larry said, lifting his head. "For my wife."

"What is?" you asked, staring at him, wanting to shake him in his chair. "You took my place here, so I've got yours."

Months passed. Years, reckoned by the blooming of plants — the ocotillo by the gate, the yucca bending down, the gaudy faces of sunflowers in the ditches — and you wondered why you were here at all, tied to a stranger who seemed to waken only at night when you went to bed, a stranger whose fingers repelled you.

One evening you went out and rode Naja into the mouth of the sun. You rode to the track and let him run free, the way you did with the colts you trained. He needed no urging, thrust himself forward like a bird and flew, so fast you couldn't count the markers, could only hold on, blinded by his mane in your face.

"Whose horse is that?" Cy Epperson asked

when you drew up.

"Mine," you said, knowing you had wanted him to discover you, had planned it in some dark corner of your body. "Mine. I raised him."

"Best leave him here. We'll train him with the rest."

"I can't pay." You couldn't see his face in the twilight, only the shape of his head against the sky.

"Pay me when he wins," Cy said, and you heard laughter in his voice. "Let's cool him off. Then I'll drive you home." He was young, good to look at, with white teeth and flashing eyes.

"I'd better walk," you said. Hope was in you, and it needed the coolness of night, the farewell songs of larks for strength.

You needed strength, for at home Larry questioned you, forced you, held you down, and took you hard and hurting as if to prove you his property.

You tasted blood on your lip, your tongue. "If you touch me again, I'll kill you," you said, wondering what had happened to that girl who had dared to hope, to the man whose eyes had once held the sky.

He reached out a hand as if to hold you off. "Now wait," he said. "A husband's got rights."

That made you laugh. "So does a wife," you said. "Think about that." You pulled your knees up to your chin, guarded yourself, and watched him pace the room, his movements awkward.

When he stopped and turned to you, his face

was cold. "Your trouble is, you think you wear the pants around here. You ever think about that?"

"Every day of my rotten life. And jumping me won't change it." You hurt in places you'd forgotten. There would be bruises on your skin come morning, more sliced into your heart.

"Bitch," he said. He sounded like you'd hit him. You wished you had.

"I'll kill you," you said again. Your hands curled into claws told you it was true.

"Bitch." The sound echoed in your head. You had no defense against his weakness.

In the morning he was gone, your money with him, and, although you watched the road for a few days, he didn't come home again.

After a while you walked a little straighter, swinging your braid. You caught yourself singing now and again. Behind the mask of your face, you began to plan, hoarding your money, hiding it in the earth behind the chicken house, dreaming it in your sleep touched by the moon.

You smiled at Cy. Around him your body rippled like a stream, but you stayed remote, giving hunger a chance to grow. And this, too, you did at a distance from yourself. You were two women — Marvel Bird, the guardian of the other who was waiting to be born.

Sometimes you questioned yourself, but not too hard. It was better not to think, better to be moved by the feel of air, the tug of the moon, voices that never lied but kept their promises year after year.

This year the summer rains came in the spring. The pastures turned green, the horses fat. Naja was sleek, muscled, three years old. Beneath you he ran easily, like the wind.

"He'll win," Cy said. "By God, he will." Cy was packing for his trip to the races, and you were helping, trying not to look as the trunks filled. You were trying not to look at Cy's back in the blue shirt, or at how his hair curled on his neck.

When you didn't answer, he looked up, reading your eyes as easily as you read signs of weather. "What are you going to do while I'm gone?" he asked.

You shrugged, tried to smile. "Keep an eye on things. Maybe get a job down at the beauty parlor."

He stood up, his face level with yours. "You, sticking your hands into old ladies' hair. I'll be damned if I'll let you."

You said: "You sound like Larry. Don't do this. Don't do that. I do what I have to." Then you wanted to cut off your tongue.

You walked away, stood by the water tank, and looked down into the dark water where your face swam, calling for help, where a white moth floated, a lost flower, on the surface. "Alone," they said. "Alone." Then Cy's face merged with yours, and the calling stopped, sinking to the bottom like a stone.

"Come with me," he said. "Naja needs you. I need you."

You knew what you needed, or the other Marvel did. Inside you she was kicking out, shoving to be born. You said: "I'm afraid."

"Don't shut out living," he said.

Inside you hands were clapping. Leaves stirred. Inside you were birdsong and a pain where your heart beat in its cage. You felt the bones around it, brittle and bending, while outside the world flowed like a stream toward an end.

In his eyes, dark as tank water, you saw yourself on the edge of dreaming. "Where is living?" you asked him. "Is it inside or out?"

He shook his head. A smile tugged at his mouth as if he were amused and trying to hide it. "Both, I guess," he said. "But that's up to you. To the person."

He put his hands on you, and you moved to meet him, feeling that you'd come to a rock midstream, that you could hold to it a while and let the water rush around you.

"I'll come, then," you said. Or maybe it was the other Marvel Bird who said the words, and who remembered the moth. Stooping, she lifted it with her finger and let it rest there, drying its wings.

Acknowledgements

As always, my thanks to my husband, Glenn G. Boyer, for his patience and his vast and flawless knowledge of history; to Lyman L. Hanley and Lyman B. Hanley, nephew and grandnephew of Louisa Houston Earp, for their invaluable recollections and assistance and their always cheerful presence; to Nebraska poet Don Welch who, years ago, took me to watch the migrating cranes and taught me about the Platte River; and to my agent and editor, Jon Tuska, whose encouragement and subtle wit keep me writing and thinking.

About the Author

Born and raised near Pittsburgh, Pennsylvania, Jane Candia Coleman majored in creative writing at the University of Pittsburgh but stopped writing after graduation in 1960 because she knew she "hadn't lived enough, thought enough, to write anything of interest." Her life changed dramatically when she abandoned the East for the West in 1986, and her creativity came truly into its own. *The Voices of Doves* (1988) was written soon after she moved to Tucson. It was followed by a book of poetry, *No Roof But Sky* (1990), and by a truly remarkable short story collection that amply repays reading and re-reading, *Stories From Mesa Country* (1991). Her short story, "Lou" in *Louis L'Amour Western Magazine* (3/94), won the Spur Award from the Western Writers of America as did her later short story, "Are You Coming Back, Phin Montana?" in *Louis L'Amour Magazine* (1/96). She has also won three Western Heritage Awards from the National Cowboy Hall of Fame. *Doc Holliday's Woman* (1995) was her first novel and one of vivid and extraordinary power. The highly acclaimed *Moving On: Stories of the West* was her first **Five Star Western**, and it contains her two Spur award-winning stories. It was followed in 1998 with the novel, *I, Pearl Hart*. It can be said that a story by Jane Candia Coleman embodies the essence of what is finest in the Western story, intimations of hope, vulnerability, and courage, while she plummets to the depths of her characters, conjuring moods and imagery with the consummate artistry of an accomplished poet.

W